SCARS

AND

BLACK

ARMOR

Scars and Black Armor is published under Reverie, a sectionalized division under Di Angelo Publications, Inc.

REVERIE

Reverie is an imprint of Di Angelo Publications.
Copyright 2021.
All rights reserved.
Printed in United States of America.

Di Angelo Publications
4265 San Felipe #1100
Houston, Texas 77027

Library of Congress
Scars and Black Armor
ISBN: 978-1-955690-06-5

Words: Liam Chambers
Cover Design: Savina Deinova
Interior Design: Kimberly James
Managing Editor: Cody Wootton
Editors: Ashley Crantas, Elizabeth Geeslin Zinn, Stephanie Yoxen

Downloadable via Kindle, Nook, and Google Play.

1. Fiction --- Fantasy --- Historical
2. Fiction --- Fantasy --- Military
3. Fiction --- Fairy Tales, Folk Tales, Legends & Mythology
4. Fiction --- War & Military
5. Fiction --- World Literature --- Greece

United States of America with int. distriution

SCARS AND BLACK ARMOR

LIAM CHAMBERS

For my father,
who willingly picked up the heaviest parts of life.

"WE MUST REMEMBER THAT ONE MAN IS MUCH THE SAME AS ANOTHER, AND THAT HE IS BEST WHO IS TRAINED IN THE SEVEREST SCHOOL."

-THUCYDIDES

.

CONTENTS

I

THE LAST OF THE MYRMIDONS

The dead men with the black armor stood in line, waiting for Charon. In their right hands, they held coins, forged of gold, but which held no monetary worth. In their left hands they held their scarred, black helmets. They did not speak as they stood, though their eyes met and quickly turned away. Falling ash made no mark on their armor; it merely blackened it further. Their time to gather onto the boat approached and the men, in silence, reflected on the choices they had made in life. Charred earth lay beneath their sandals, and drops of blood remained, staining the ground where they had fallen. But the earth lay still now. Though their bodies remained, they were not truly there. The men, unbound by the rules of the earth and the laws of Hades shuffled across the hard ground. As Charon's boat slid onto the river's bank, they stepped forth to be ferried to the golden fields, eager to meet the ones that they had loved and protected.

As he had done in life, the officer with the scruffy black hair stood in the final place in line. Shuffling his gold coin nervously in his palm, he followed the marching line of the dead. But the boatman, whose duty it was to bring them across the Styx and Acheron, raised his bony fingers towards the sky and motioned for him to stop, indicating that the man who had sacrificed the most would not be joining his brothers in arms. Charon curled his fingers and pointed to the vast mountain of Olympus located behind the man, and with a deft push, steered the friends and brothers out to the river, leaving the single warrior on the shores of Greece. The last Myrmidon cast his coin onto the ground, where it fell softly, cushioned by the burnt powder. In his heart, the warrior knew he would no longer have need of such things.

The mountain called to him.

From the shore he watched as the water of the Styx gently rolled against the departing skiff. The boat, made of stripped pine, moved ahead, sending trails of auburn like rusted metal down the river as it passed. At his feet the calm water reflected his heart, yet the dark ripples resonating from the boat moved like creatures from the deep.

Marching alone along the dark path, the man thought deeply on his life. Long before his arrival, the footsteps of others had compacted the dirt road. Snaking from the beach to the open canvas of the forest he followed the winding trail. He noticed that the green, summer limbs of the trees he had known well in life were but falling ash, black as a thief's cloak. Above him, the mountain loomed. With each step he took, the crest of the peak swallowed more of the sky, and soon, the shadow of the beast engulfed his black armor in darkness. Pausing just before the threshold of the climb, he breathed in and felt the cold air fill his lungs, knowing that once he reached for the first rock, it had begun, and no retreat would be permissible. Steadying his feet on the small boulders which had crumbled from the ridges above, the warrior studied the path. An impossible distance. But not to him. Not to this man. It was only impossible if he believed it so.

The man upon the hill chose which rock to grab, carefully.

Only the most watchful eye, passing below the peak, might catch a glimpse of him. He climbed judiciously, but with strength. There was no stopping for comfort. He climbed, though the sinews of the muscles in his back throbbed with pain when they pushed against the leather straps of his armor. But he was brave in the fact that he merely continued. Days passed between handholds. Years waned along ridges. Centuries tore through the world of men below with each precipice the warrior overcame. The man still climbed, though he could not see his aim. It was only when the man crested a shallow ridge did his view open to expose the temple, still sitting far above in the distance. It was at this moment that he noticed the other climbers. Men camped along the route, some moved slowly with dread, but their faces meant nothing to the Myrmidon. The men recognized each other as warriors only by the state of their armor.

One man wore the trinkets and adornments of a vast empire, and yet he was so young, hardly older than thirty. His gaze was endless—it searched the land below, yearning for more.

Another man wore sheets of iron. Woven in a manner unfamiliar to the climbing Myrmidon, they bore three gold lions in the center of his cherry breastplate.

The final man was elderly, but a colossus in stature, and he wore a cloak of crimson; his eyes alone could stop armies. His bronze shield bore the Greek letter *lambda*, and he spoke but one word to the warrior in black. *Andreia*. Courage, or fortitude. In return, the Myrmidon uttered one word, *Phrater*, which means kinsman, or brother, before continuing his ascent up the mountain.

The Myrmidon continued to do his duty in death as he had in life, and not once did his eyes meet the ground far below. With his world in his hands, his heart drove each grasp, but he did not consider how high he would need to climb. He only considered the next decision, the next correct route to take.

The man continued up the slope, ascending to the holy glimmer of the heavens. Mount Olympus. And, as he reached the ancient temple and saw Zeus, the giant figure cast a great shadow upon the hall. A warm evening breeze curled around the white pillars and sang through the halls as the god beckoned him to approach. Mountain seamlessly melded with earth and the sanctuary sang with grace as the wind whistled through the architecture. Never before had the warrior seen such grandeur or opulence. He had spent his life atop soil and rock.

When the Myrmidon finally arrived at the end of the hall, he kneeled before the great god Zeus. Flames reflected from his armor against candlelit galleries of Olympus. Zeus sat silent as the man approached the throne of marble.

And outside the window, white swallows swung carelessly and surfed the breeze. Clouds drifted across the blood-red sky as the waning sun made camp beyond the horizon. Fractured red light fell through the windows and scattered upon the wall of the mountain fortress.

His armor, unlike the others who had made their stories known on the mountain, was plain. No gold adorned the steel; no medals hung upon his breast, nor commendations upon his sleeve. He did not need those merits of bravery. Proof of his courage was in the scars that etched his armor, which ran like streams throughout his various gear. And his valor spoke. It spoke through the scarred valleys of his shield. Fire molded his mettle. His arms, steady from the burden of combat, kept his helmet firmly mounted in his left hand.

He was a Myrmidon. One of the ant-men.

The warrior kept his head bowed until the god addressed him. Zeus had created all, including Ares, warlord of the heavens, to whom this man had pledged his identity long ago.

Still kneeling, the man remained still. Zeus broke the silence of the mountain, with a voice that tore the very fabric of the air.

"Here, young soldier, I have called you to confront you, so that you may recount the morals of your actions — the consequences of your chaos.

"I summon few warriors to climb the treacherous slope. But when I do, I expect that they will choose their grips carefully. In their hands, they put their trust in the crumbling stones, as they make their way to judgement."

Zeus leaned back upon his throne.

"The stones themselves judge each movement, each life, and some stories they deem

unworthy to tell. It matters, above all things, which stone they grab, and which stone crumbles under their grip.

"The stones know more than the man does of himself. And though a man reaches and strives for the peak of the mountain, he does so with hope in his heart, and with the weight of his armor on his back."

Zeus, appearing as a towering god above the halls, took his place above the man in question. With sharp words, like barbs, his voice was a storm which rumbled and echoed throughout the artwork.

"Tell me your story," Zeus commanded, his arm outstretched and his palm facing up.

Gently placing his sword and shield on the cold floor, the officer stood up with his back straight and his chest high, though his body ached. His eyes, black as an obsidian sea, shone in the god's light. "Though it is long, and full of suffering, I was but a soldier... I lived a soldier's life," replied the hollow voice of the Myrmidon.

Zeus paused.

"And this suffering, was it of the soldier, or of the man?"

"It was the suffering of both," the Myrmidon replied. "Of the soldier's spirit that develops from the broken soul of man. My experience of love and hate and of war is universal, and cruel."

Zeus nodded in agreement. "But the man who picks up his sword and shield, when asked, he knows a different part of the earth."

The god continued.

"The man who does not, however, will forever in the caverns of his heart know that no matter how great a life he lived, no matter how ferociously he loved, and no matter how professional his career, he fell short of a mark"

Zeus contemplated this before continuing, allowing his words to echo.

"He yearns, because he knows that no matter how astute his political observations, no matter how close he felt to the gods in his philosophy, he will still, on the cold stone of his deathbed and before the long night takes him away, reflect, and notice a gap in the things he could have done. He never put on the line that which is absolute: his life. He never had to hold his dying brother and reassure him that all will be fine, watch *the light fade from his eyes and take its place in the midnight sky. Those who remain die in peace, but peace of the external while the storm rages within. I watched you perform these acts, but I also watched as you left him there, where his blood mixed with the scorched sand of the battlefield. I watched as you walked to the nearby stream and you washed his life from your hands and helmet, and I saw how your eyes followed the crimson veins of the washed blood in the river as they drifted away."*

The Myrmidon's head bowed a touch further. The god persisted.

"And later I watched as you sat quietly in the dawn, in times of peace, near a different but all too familiar stream, which burned blue, like diamond, but which harbored the same quiet desperation as before."

As the Myrmidon stood quickly, his eyes betrayed his stoic image. In the corners of the warrior's eyes, his muscles contracted with the pain of memory.

Zeus continued.

"The river held the worst kind of desperation: the kind that nestles deep within the muscles of a warrior's back, which knots, and sleeps there. Only those who are left know this. But the man who avoids this responsibility, the one of war, expires with the knowledge that death will reveal the truth of his life; he will know that there were heavier things he could have picked up but chose not to. Things like the sword. The shield made of hardened oak. The weight of the dead. But of all these powerful things, he will not know the heaviest: the weight of a small child's hand placed softly in his. He will only understand the absence of hope and guidance he could have given to a soul. He never gave a piece of himself to those desperate for faith and happiness.

"But you, you were able to push the dark thoughts of yourself far enough down, so that your knowledge of the malevolence of the world did not show through your eyes and corrupt. You could do this because you acquainted yourself with those heavy things. You needed to perform the impossible: to laugh and smile and play but to always remember the blood in the river. The great dichotomy of all things—of life and of death."

The man replied, "These desperations I carry here in my heart, they are mine to keep. They are the charge of men. And I must apologize, Zeus, for I am a modest soldier. I cannot, though I would cherish the ability, begin to speak like the gods. I know the world through my simple lens, my simple life. I will explain to you the things I have learned but I will not be able to do so like the great philosophers of our time. Perhaps, it should have been them meeting you, god of gods, rather than me."

Zeus answered,. *"I know these desperations, Myrmidon. I bear them in my heart also — the hearts of gods feel the same sting as that of mortals. We feel the same intimate pain, of family and of loss. Though we are eternal, it only means that we contend with these things for much longer. It only means that we are given more time to resolve that which cannot be resolved, for neither the hearts of men nor gods have the capacity to do so."*

The Myrmidon's voice wavered. "What, then, should I have done? Should I have loved with less passion? Prayed with less piety? Killed… with less remorse?"

"No," replied the god. *"From Mount Olympus I watched, and though I only saw your actions, you lived honorably. Tell me, though, how does a mortal carry himself in such a way through these painful trials?"*

The Myrmidon was silent. Deep in thought, he questioned the violent life he had led.

Finally, the soldier replied. Some fragment of wisdom returned, granted to him by a mentor, so long ago.

"He endures. And he listens, above all, to that which guides his heart."

Zeus confronted the Myrmidon's first apprehension.

"Time is what we have then, and it is a creation of the gods, so I have much time to listen. Tell me the story of your life, and recount to me the lessons you learned in your mortal experience. Tell the god of all gods all the hardships that men must undertake. From Olympus we saw, but we may never understand. It is true — the men in black are a creation of mine, but I am torn by fate and time; did I alleviate the sorrows of mortals by creating these men, or did I create more heartache? That, my son, is why you are here."

II

WE LEFT ONLY OURSELVES BEHIND

I was born on a small island off the Greek coast. We lived in poverty, cloaked beneath a faceless tyrant. Orphaned wards of the city-state, we were put to work as soon as our tiny hands could hold a spade or pick — often sooner. There was little direction in our work, only the simple tasks we needed to finish, and the anger of the two grown men who worked the farm. They had been soldiers who, when war erupted, had abandoned their brothers from Mycenae. For their cowardice, the ruler banished them to this island and put them in charge of the farm. They unleashed their demons of self-loathing upon us boys. They were not good men; they fell victim to those base emotions which plague lesser souls. They had grown in these very fields, and their minds were twisted, full of nettles and choked with bracken.

I remember nothing about childhood but the cold grasses of the fields and the roar of the sea, distant and unseen, yet loud like thunder. At night, the men did not bother to lock the barn, for we had no place to escape to.

We could not leave. Our prison of labor was brutal, though, we knew no different. One night, the gate that locked the paddock of cattle blew open in the midst of a storm. Locking the gate which housed the herd was a task of mine, and so as punishment I stood in the howling wind and pelting rain for the rest of the night, with only livestock for company. And when I reentered the barn the following day after work, my frozen and blistered hands ached, my blood immobilized from the chill. I shook for hours. Another boy prepared me a warm vat until the blood in my body began to move again. His name eludes me, but he was kind, and would often offer me crumbs of his own bread. My own work with the cattle often left me hungrier than the others. And it made no difference, the bread, but the gesture was generous. The following month, however, they tied him to a post and whipped his back until the bones of his spine poked through his skin, all for spilling cheap seeds. He died on the post, and they left him for the wolves. After that, I began sharing my own bread.

In early spring, I was tending the crops and walking the edge of one of our fields. The owners had only recently stopped whipping us. For the most part, we had proven our ability to work and complete the simple tasks needed, but the marks on my back were still raw and open, and often they would bleed by the end of the day for lack of rest. This day, though, was worse than any whipping I'd ever received; its cruelty would haunt me for the rest of my life.

The previous night, the gods sent a furious rain. The mud surrounding our farm was deep and sticky, like clay. In one misstep while circling the farm, I lost my footing in the mud and tumbled down to the ditch that functioned as the runoff for our land. I landed hard on my back. My lungs convulsed and screamed for air. I was in a pit, stuck in the sludge and in pain. The mud invaded the open wounds upon my back. And as I wiped the mud from my eyes, I saw the snakes.

The blood called to them.

Their scales were the black of a starless sky, striped with a dark red like the deep padding of the muscles in the boy's back who'd died on the post.

The serpents went mad with bloodlust; their eyes turned crimson as the running blood from my back enraged their senses. As I attempted to writhe myself free from the mud, they latched their sharp fangs onto my legs and arms. *I will die in this pit,* I thought. The last thing I would see would be the cold amber eyes as they consumed my flesh.

But I did not die. I know only that one of my colleagues pulled me from the pit and saved me, but I lost all consciousness. In the weeks following, during my bedridden recovery, I awoke many nights in a terror. Under my sheets and my clothes and under the tight layers of my skin I saw them slithering, and I was powerless to fight them.

As boys, we did not grow until we left. But when we left, we grew up far too quickly. The Myrmidons told us that we descended from the ants, and that you, Zeus, had made us into warriors.

When we found ourselves at the darkest part of our young lives, the men with black armor came for us.

We matured, as tends to happen as a result of one's environment. Although most of what I remember after growing is war and pain, there was love also. I know no date of when I left, nor season of when they saved us. It could have been spring when the wildflowers bloomed. Possibly it was when the winter rain began to fall. I have no feeling from that place — no tactile memories of the land. No smells return to me. I remember only pain and dealing with heartache.

Later I found heartache again, but it was of a different form, for there are many types. I knew the great Achilles. We laughed together as children. We bled together as men. We destroyed ourselves together, though in separate ways. And so, these details I will share with you.

But I fear I have fallen short of a full life, and of a full commitment to family and children. Though I tried my best to love and to sacrifice for others, I was just a soldier. And I plead for you, Zeus, to have mercy, and to not judge me on that which I longed for but never achieved — a life of love.

Before death, we saw the world and the evil in it, but we lived our lives with discipline and with sense. We stuck to our code as much as we could, but its pressure fractured some of us. Every man knows that to truly live, even the strictest of rules must bend… These things I will share though they pain me greatly to do so.

"All men are shattered in some way," replied Zeus.

A darkness enveloped the bright eyes of the soldier. "This tale is more about what we lived for, and what we died in spite of."

Until I became one of them, I knew nothing of why they altered our fate. But we knew our rulers, and our tyrant, and we knew that the Myrmidons took our island by force, with pure violence. So many men died that night that the stacked bodies formed bridges across the river.

No level of persuasion or rhetoric would have been ample to convince the oppressive ruler of our land. This happens with the powerful and the corrupt. These qualities often align in our world. Instead of language, the Mymridons had war. Instead of negotiation, there was only assault.

The night they came for us, the river stole the blood from the dead men. In the sunset I saw the water return to the earth, bringing the blood with it. The fallen men brought a restoration to the arteries of the island.

The red river drowned the lives of men who had lost their way.

And we left.

The Myrmidons gave us choice, for the first time in our young yet brutal lives — although in truth, there was only one possibility. They needn't have asked us if we wanted to leave. None of us would stay; we had nearly nothing to our names, and hate was our one familiarity. Even if we did remain, our hearts would never settle. The farmers whipped us. They beat us like cattle. We slept little, worked always, and they thrashed us even when we worked hard. Our cracked hands were small and purple. Our empty stomachs ached as badly as our broken bodies. Our shattered spirits prayed to the stars. So, what boy would not want to become a Myrmidon? These warriors commanded the earth they stood upon. Sand seemed to part only for their feet. Waves seemed only to cascade in the direction their ships yearned to go. Wind only howled in the direction that took them towards the sounds of death.

"Come," said one, stretching his hand toward me. His body bore the same scarring as his armor, and his eyes, though hard as polished marble, held some measure of sympathy.

And we parted from our island with the slow dusk. We could have stayed broken, or we could leave, and become one of them — the men with the black armor. The road, we knew even then, would not be easy.

We boarded a ship made of oak. Twenty men sat cleaning their gear. They dipped the blood-soaked armor into the sea. As I stepped aboard the boat, the gentle rocking unnerved me. After a few minutes, I wanted to vomit, but it could've been my nerves.

But the ship was massive — it loomed like a behemoth in the calm night. Iron strappings held the parallel pieces of the wood together. Sat atop the bow was a black spear, which cut the spray of the ocean, and when the wind hit the edge of the metal, it sang to us. We would, in time, come to see that all Myrmidon spears are sharp enough to shear the mist itself, even the "dead pikes" — instruments of violence that fell when their Myrmidon masters died in battle. Dead pikes lined the handrails of the ships. It was a constant reminder of creed, culture, and proximity, to death and life. Even the ones that lined the burning pyres of the dead warriors in the funeral games were deadly. You would not find a single spear or weapon of warfare not prepared for death.

As we crossed the threshold of the oak boat, there was a single boy already there. He was not from our island. Silently, he sat in the corner like a stowaway. His blonde hair flowed in the wind, but his blue eyes were full of pain. Like us, he held immense fear for what lay ahead. We knew he was one of us because he was angry inside. His eyes stayed low as we walked past him. His body shook with the cold. But when I sat down next to him, he still shared his blanket with me.

One warrior, whose black shield was strewn across his back, and who carried an ash-crafted spear in his right hand, stepped forward from the shadows. He addressed me directly.

"What shall it be, boy, destiny or history?" he asked.

"Destiny," I said though I had no grasp of the concept, but I said it all the same, because it felt like the right thing to do. And all the Myrmidons rapped the butts of their spears against the hard deck of the ship. It echoed into the night as one sound. One deafening resonance of daring men.

Another thrust a lit torch into my hands.

"Then the island must be your tablet and the flame your scribe. Burn it to the ground," he ordered.

I walked, alone, while the Myrmidons and the boys watched from the ships. I unlocked the paddocks that held the livestock, as had been my job, and let the animals run free, watching them disappear into the night's liberty. With purpose, I touched the flame to the dried wood of the barn, and soon, the crackling splinters had turned the entire farm into an inferno. Our childhood and the pain it had inflicted burned to ash and rubble in a matter of minutes.

Turning my back to the blaze I started towards the boats. The heat, now my unquestionable ally, guided me towards destiny and with a fiery gust the sparks from my past life blew into the night's sky.

We sailed away from the island with the Myrmidons. In the silence of the sea, the warrior spoke again to us. "Close your eyes. Breathe deeply and let the brisk touch of the ocean breeze fill your lungs. Remember now until your death, that each breath is a gift. At every moment, we may depart this world without warning. How will men think of you when you are gone? Let your mortality and vulnerability guide your actions and your thoughts, and take each moment; someday, we will have our final one. You there," he again addressed me, "can you control the sea?"

"No, sir," I said.

"Can you control the gale?"

"No, sir."

"Can you control flame, earth, or sky?"

"No, sir."

"Then accept these things into your heart and maintain authority over that which you can control in this life. Once you overcome that voice, all anxiety and doubt will strip away like bark from a fading pine, leaving your soul free."

Our camp was set up on an island between the sea and the mountains, the lowest and highest points our eyes could see. We learned our place between the falcons and the shoreline, and in doing so we equalized the ground we called our home.

We had no knowledge of hell or of gods. We knew only what we saw. This was the immaturity of our youth.

Nestled in our small corner of the world, the Myrmidons taught us freedom, but true freedom — freedom through strict self-restraint and through the sovereign claim of one's soul. To help us reclaim our souls, they placed wooden weapons in our hands. Though the wood weighed down our arms, the mock weapons weren't lethal. Still, the oak left its bruises and its marks upon us.

We were not yet warriors, not even adults. There was much to prove before we received our black shields.

It was not the sharpening of the sword, but of the mind.

The men would tell us this, in time.

And each of us brought a few things from our island; we owned next to nothing, but we brought the trinkets and the trivial things to our new lives. We held them closely to our hearts to remind us of what we could now never return to.

It struck me — the meaning each boy had placed on the items he'd found in the dirt. One boy had a broken piece of pottery, which depicted a rearing stallion. Another found the feathered fletching of an old arrow, from wars long past. I myself had a fragment of fabric, a piece of sail which I had found in the sand. At night I had dreamed of it as part of a whole, a small ship that would take me far away. But back on our island, each of us had taken the time to hide our secret things. Our treasures hid in the walls, in our beds, or in places in the fields to keep them hidden from the tyrants of men. We owned something, and so we protected it, and we risked our own safety for these worthless things.

They were valueless, and important.

In the distance, monoliths of stone surged from the earth and reached forever for the heavens. The lush green flora was compact and dense, and the small pieces of earth — the carved trails and camps — came from this beauty for the use of the Myrmidons. Carefully, the paths followed the land. We learned later that the Myrmidons sought the approval of Artemis. Our footprints on the earth were small and inconsequential. The island was no bigger than our old one, but it was far denser with life. It held secrets ours never could. Buried beneath its forest was hope.

They gave us blankets to sleep under. We had never seen such things before. The cots were comfortable. The Myrmidons spoke of nothing that night; they let us rest. One of the men patted me on the shoulder as I lay my head down to sleep, and I was overcome with emotion. I wept underneath the blanket.

In the dark of that first night, our faint heartbeats rose and fell together. In the same tent, we slept in beds made of straw, and we had undergone the same hardships in life; this made us feel equal. Somehow the air felt heavier, and yet easier to breathe. We were nervous but we did not dread the morning as we had before. We felt our lives had changed, but we did not yet know exactly how.

We had all, excluding the boy with blonde hair, come from the same tyranny. I knew not his origin, and he did not speak to me about it for a long time.

But we heard whispers on the wind.

We awoke the next morning to beckoning outside the tent. Three mentors presented themselves. The rest of the Myrmidons had disappeared in the night. We stood in silence along the beach and stared at the men. From the shores, the walls rose. Jagged layers of stone, moved by the gods surrounded us. The outer level of sandstone had rusted a gentle tone of bronze from years of combat with the sea.

We whispered to each other. The squawk of seagulls filled the air above us. They circled above our heads.

"You see the tall man, with the blue eyes, there on the left? Those eyes have fury in them…" one boy breathed.

Another chimed in. "That one with long brown hair, he seems less menacing. But he demands something unsaid…"

"What about him?" I whispered, nodded towards the third man. "The one with the scar across his left chin. He seems peaceful. Why does it disturb me?"

Deimos, god of Terror.

Teris, god of Liberation.

Iesos, god of Salvation.

Each of these men lived up to their namesakes. Though mortal blood flowed through their veins, they had the bearings of the fearsome gods we would come to know.

Unlike our farmers, these men possessed no cruelty. They did not begrudge the sun its dawning, nor were they harsh for the sake of obedience. Instead of the senseless violence of the farmers, these men stood tall and quiet in the morning breeze. Only Deimos paced back and forth before our ranks like a caged lion. We stood because we existed in the moment; they stood with intent.

We slouched in our crooked line, darting nervous glances at the men and the sea. The line we had created was not ordered, nor organized, merely made out of habit, as we knew to line up on the farm before the workday started. The sun, now beating down upon our sweating brows, glimmered on the sea and on the black shields, and we said nothing.

Deimos approached, and as he did, I felt as though he walked only towards me, as if all the other boys disappeared.

It was solely he and I on the beach.

"Move," he said, his voice raspy and grizzled. He grabbed my shoulders as he directed me towards the front of the line.

His hands were iron. When they wrapped around my upper arms, my body moved as if caught in the power of the ocean tides, and when I became still again the other boys reappeared. Now I could see the spidery waterways of scars that damaged his armor. These unnamed deeds spoke more to me than his words, which were few.

In my childhood I knew how to respect out of fear or cruelty, but even as a boy I knew that this kind of reverence was vastly different. This was a respect of character, and of the intangible shadow he cast upon the sand.

Deimos and Teris organized us by some method, unknown to me, but by what they saw in our gazes. They could see something in us, even then, that which we could not see in ourselves, and this gave us hope. Most children simply need an adult to believe in them.

The warriors stared at each boy until they made their decision. Iesos recorded whispered judgements on parchment about each of us as they did so. When they had finished, they gave the rest of the day to us so that we could organize our spaces, take care of our gear, and prepare ourselves for the following day.

That night we sat on our cots and looked worriedly at one another, and we said nothing.

But there was a feeling we all shared.

There on that beach, we gave thanks for no palaces, no kingdoms, no dictators. We lived in our kingdom of heaven, no gods or rulers but the warriors at our side. With them, we learned the ways of hard and noble living. That night, after a lifetime trudging through unfair law and oppression, we slept beneath the stars, which made us feel free, and alive.

The blonde boy looked at us too, but he was anxious in our company, and he went to bed earlier than the rest of us. Judging by his face I guessed he was only a harvest or two younger than I. In the night I could see the whites of his eyes. Under the Greek moon, I was certain that sleep eluded him. It evaded me like a shadow as well.

Determined to find out about him, I asked about his life. He told me only that his name was Achilles. His voice was soft as it flowed on the breeze. There was pain there, nestled deep in his chest. But he pushed it far down in order to be compassionate to me.

And on that beach, a new foundation from which to build ourselves emerged.

And because of our robbed childhoods, we would differ from the people we'd meet later in life. We excelled because our early existences and refuge took root in the dark. Instead of fear, the black armor of the Myrmidons comforted us. We had no knowledge that children should turn to the light for comfort, as the cruelty of man had taken these things from us. When we finally laid our eyes to rest, and although we were cold and sore by the day's end, the night was our sanctuary. Allowed now to reinvent ourselves, we drifted off to sleep and, for the first time in our lives, we felt part of something worth living for. Awakening the next morning, we realized that we must forge our new identities in our minds; nothing at all had changed about us. But the men we now looked up to were different, and that would alter almost everything we thought we knew.

Our clothes, armor, and false weapons were tattered and ragged. We assembled our gear. Deimos unceremoniously shoved it towards us. He had decided to prove that, to him, we did not merit such honors.

The next day he gave us our first taste of true discipline.

Deimos' anger ripped through the tent. The standards put forth by Teris were not achieved that day, though later, Deimos' temper raged even when they were. When Deimos left each morning, our possessions lay strewn across the ground. When we despaired, Iesos calmly explained that "we all must trust in the word of the gods." His words grabbed us by the shoulders and picked us up from where we sat in the mud.

Iesos moved his hands in strange ways as he spoke, as if he was toying with unseen wisps of smoke. His words always referenced the powers of the pantheon. Although I listened fervently, sometimes I had little clue of what he was saying or what he meant.

Teris was the opposite of Deimos. He was not lenient, but rather he was demanding in the way that a serene sea still demands a sturdy vessel, and he was unwavering in his calm nature. After these sessions, Teris would lead us out of the cramped tent and into the mountains to strengthen our bodies. He spoke always in the same tone — collected, and his words were simple. His smooth voice never fell victim to the pitches of emotion or worry. His anger never surfaced, and his philosophy was free of the divine. In each moment he was present with the world.

And it was in that moment of clarity where I first understood Teris that I also noticed the qualities of the boys who accompanied me on my journey. Some were naturally quick; some could lace the leather of their armor tight, without issue. My hands struggled to find the balance and the strength, and my legs would burn up far before theirs did. My lungs seemed to burst while theirs breathed steady. Of the many boys who had decided to become warriors, I felt like the most ordinary.

And I hated lacing my gear. The natural skill eluded me, and as I pulled the ties my fingertips would often slip and tear the skin. The burning in my hands continued long into the night and disrupted the little sleep I could get. When it was time to lace the gear again the wounds would only worsen.

Leandros was extraordinarily tall. His reach far outstretched ours. We always left with bruises from combat with him, but he lacked the ability to know when to cease. Even in times of relative peace his hands shook. When unexpected liberty to complete a task arose, Leandros was the boy who would work the hardest and get the least done. I liked him because he was tough, but he needed friends who could draw the line for him, at the right moment.

Kristos was quiet, but faster than any other across the slippery sand. On powerful and nimble legs, he snaked his way behind his opponents before the dust had settled. None could catch him, though he struggled in many other tasks.

Alexius was the light in the darkness. When I struggled, he was there to guide and then to tease. When my mind wandered, he steadied the ship of my insecurity. I loved him like a brother. I cherished every minute I had on the earth with such a loyal and worthy warrior. It is how all men should strive to be — how all men should remember those closest to them. Though he was shorter than most, he performed his physical duties to a high, if not higher standard than the rest. Only Pyrros bested him at the grounds. But Alexius had one quality that I never owned during my time on the physical earth — he could make anyone, including the serious men instructing us, laugh. He did this in the worst possible situations. A soldier lives and dies on dark humor, and when those who harness and hone this skill are gone, the void is unfillable.

He was never serious — he channeled his seriousness into his poetry. It was a quality that as boys we derided, but as men we loved. We came to realize that there was nothing weak about the process of writing, but rather it was a direct route to the hearts of warriors.

I found him most days scribbling words onto parchment; his only company was the sea.

"May I read it?" I asked him one evening.

He smiled. "It is no thing worth reading," he replied.

"All the same, may I read it?"

"Maybe one day, my friend." He laughed.

There was another boy, Hypatios, whose intellect was sharper than the rest. He switched his grip mid-battle, knowing the sequences of war from both angles, and practiced swordcraft only with his weaker left hand. He subjected himself to more bruises by this choice. He suffered retribution from the instructors, but when he had mastered both grips, he was unstoppable in close-quarters combat.

There were many others, each who had their own exceptional quality.

But there was one boy who stood far ahead of all the others in his physical strength: Pyrros. Because of his indisputable strength, he dominated the camp. And he was unkind, as most powerful and rough men tend to be. When Hypatios took an open bed, Pyrros, acting as some deranged disciple of Deimos, sent his equipment flying across the tent. He shoved the smaller boy down hard into the sand. We knew that he would be a formidable warrior, so we kept our distance. We hoped that we would awake one morning with the same strength he so naturally possessed.

In our secluded camp we rarely saw the other Myrmidons. Though we barely knew the instructors, they consumed our lives. No mention of the main regiment emerged in our training. We knew only that it wasn't our own. But every week or so, one of these men would arrive bearing a message from the central camp.

On one of these damp, cold mornings, a Myrmidon arrived by boat and landed upon our shore. As gentle as his arrival was, he then jumped from the side of the ship toward land, which seemed to us to be an impossible distance. The impact of his boots as they landed scattered the sand with such violence that I saw the earth shift under his weight. *He must be a commander*, I thought, a leader of men. His importance radiated from the hot sand.

He delivered fresh bedding.

Teris saw that I was watching the man intently and approached. A perplexed look was cast over my face.

"Even the men who perform the menial tasks do so with unwavering resolve. Even the lowest soldier appears at all times as a warrior. He performs his duty as if he were the last warrior standing on the battleground. He does so even if that task is a mere delivery."

"So, this man is a front-ranker?"

He smiled. "Kalliaros. Commander of the second battalion. Delivering bedding himself so his men may rest with their families."

It was impossible to tell his rank from my vantage point. While our instructions told us that the Myrmidons operated under a meritorious system of generals, commanders, officers, shieldmen, and swordsmen, his armor gave us no such indication of his position. But all Myrmidons knew which part of the line they held; they respected each other's positions. Kerberos was our general then, so we were told. He was a man who had risen from the ranks.

When we trained, we trained for war but for life as well. Before we received swords, we drilled with broomstick handles. As the wood wore away with our grip, we spent our evenings prying the slivers from our fingers and our palms. We did not complain. We rejoiced in the fact that with each sliver lost, our weapons became a touch lighter, and faster in training. While we improved, our calloused hands and hardened minds made each day purposeful, and so we lived with a passion that few others experience. We lived in the grips of pursuit, which gives meaning to life above all things.

Harshness became our caregiver and pain our nursemaid; they cradled us each morning and put us away to sleep each night. It was a comfort to feel this kind of ache.

When the wood became too light, they handed us daggers. When our daggers proved too light, shields increased our load. When a boy could run the mountain path with the dagger and the shield, he received a sword. We grasped the swords. Our arms felt heavy. But we did not gripe because no boy wanted to be the first one to complain.

The ones who complained never lasted the entirety of training. We found that as a group, as a team, we strived to help each other, but when a boy began to distance himself from us, when the complaining began, it was clear that the sun would soon set upon his failures, never rise again, and he would leave. That was the power of our group, and of elimination from our ranks.

No man survives without the help of his friends and the discipline he learns from carrying the heavy things alongside those he has suffered with. No man can walk the road solo for the entirety of his journey. The boys we spent our days with carried the same things as we did. We struggled. We were stricken with doubt, and uncertainty of what the future held for us. At times we lost our temper with each other. Fistfights were a regular occurrence within the privacy of our tent. We were not punished for such things. Our emotions ran high. Though all these occurrences were a demonstration of how we dealt with our training, the boys I knew were witty, and full of laughter.

The members of our tribe understood each other. Laid bare were each boy's fears and doubts. Our friends understood these things deeper than we understood them ourselves. For that reason, our comrades constantly threw taunts and jabs towards us. Our friends chose words that, though lighthearted, cut to our bones. That is how we operated — our dark humor carried us through the days, while our discipline kept us honest through the night. But our discipline was not a consequence of our stoicism or grit. Instead, our determination was the simple result of our unity; it was the only thing we knew.

But we failed often as well, and when we failed, it stripped us down to the core, to our skeletons. Exposed for our comrades in full view were the ligaments of our heartaches and the tendons of our anguish. At first, our failures were not burdened alone, but rather as one. Only when we became a true team did our failures fall upon our individual shoulders. Until we proved that we had self-confidence and ability, we lived and died as one squad, as one unit. We relied on each other more than we relied on the sun to rise.

This was a method in which we could understand the repercussions of our failures and the impact they had upon others, and not only ourselves.

At first light, on a morning in early spring, we found ourselves at the killing ground. Lined with the trees we had felled, the square arena of sand sat quiet in the sun. Deimos had ordered us to carry the framework of the ground from the woods, months before. Alexius had fallen victim to his fatigue the night previous. He had rushed at dawn to complete his morning evolutions, and so had forgotten his left elbow guard at camp. There was no opportunity for recourse. If he pursued his error, the instructors would easily spot it. But if called to the square, the lack of protection would be obvious.

Presented with two choices — tell the truth or be hopeful that he was not summoned — he decided on the latter. But, after a match had concluded between Leandros and myself, the inevitable tides of fate rolled through. The call came.

"I have no left elbow guard," he said meekly. He wanted to laugh because of his temperament but knowing what that would mean for the rest of us he remained silent.

Deimos erupted. "You speak this now!? Only now when called!?" He was furious because he knew no matter how the Alexius responded, the absence of truth declared that the boy had already lied to him.

"At the beginning of sparring," he replied, with fear in his voice, but he had at least spoken the truth. Much good it did us.

Deimos destroyed us. Us. Not Alexius alone. Into the Aegean. Out. Blood. Spit. Crawls through the burning sand. Up the mountain. More blood. Less spit. Down the mountain.

During the tirade, we dribbled pieces of regurgitated food and sand from our mouths, and our knees buckled under the weight of his failure. Alexius struggled and Deimos piled extra armor they kept at the killing ground on the boy's back. They had plenty of additional armor in case a boy forgot his.

Deimos spoke in a furious but cackling voice, "Seems that now you have three or four elbows, boy! You are Briareos, borne of mortal flesh! No enemy shall touch you; you are far too protected! Up you go!" He pointed at the mountain and cackled, giddy with sadism.

When Alexius returned, he appeared on the verge of death, gaunt were his cheekbones and his red eyes cracked like a sunset over a sailor's sea. But, as he always had, he looked at me as I continued to vomit into the hot sand and like a child snickered, "My friend Stelios, please remind me on our next occasion that I do indeed have elbows."

I could not constrain a desperate laugh, though I did not dare let Deimos see. Alexius was in a far worse state than I, and yet his attitude never faltered. I laughed, which made the fine, powdered dust in front of me, lined with my own blood and spittle, fly back up into my lungs. And I gagged more.

When most of the boys had vomited or had dry-heaved on the beach,

Deimos left.

Teris stepped forward and spoke in the straightforward and calm manner he always had.

"Truth. It is the highest calling of Myrmidon ideals. It is the most useful tactic of war. It allows commanders to make decisions that reflect the entirety of the strategic goal. Hide the truth… men die."

None of us ever lied to them again.

When we were young on the farm, we worked, and we labored, but our tasks were our limits. Here on our island, we had tasks, but we also had unlimited potential. So, we carried all the things given to us — we were proud now to own anything at all — and when our shoulders ached under the weight of the gear, we knew that the added weight was in fact liberation.

But, in our unlimited ambitions, and in the chaos of our training, it was clear that some boys would have an easier time succeeding in the war than others, as it is in life. There is no equal playing field for those seeking the ultimate test of character; there is only dedication to succeeding.

We did the absolute best with the attributes we had, and we cultivated the qualities we thought might help us down the road. Some cultivated these qualities faster than others. Some discarded this principle completely and decided to resign themselves to remain in the same body and spirit they had always had.

These boys died slow deaths far before their hearts stopped beating.

We finally understood shared pain was a gift, something cherished, and then we started to succeed. Though it was simple to succeed, it was still not easy. And yet, they told us everything we needed to do, in excruciating detail. There were no hidden tests, nor rigged evolutions; we needed to follow the rules, tell the truth, and do each thing, no matter how small or insignificant with the same vigor.

When dusk came, we thrived. The Myrmidons held limits on when we could sleep, but not how far into the dark night we could toil. We awoke every morning at the prescribed hour. So, we took the early hours for ourselves. It was the first thing we ever owned in our lives other than our armor and the keepsakes from our island.

The mist rolled over the distant island only after the chestnut dirt had dried and flaked for days on end under the relentless sun. It happened each time the island dried to the point of comfort, and it brought with it the flood. When the rains brought the fury of the heavens upon our shoulders, we said nothing. We listened to the drops ring from the armored shoulders of our teachers. We stood, backs straight and rigid, in the midst of the downpour. Each drop burned our exposed skin, but it reminded us with each sting that we were alive. As the bones of our fingers froze, we ran like dogs to pump the blood back to our extremities, and so we controlled what we could control. Though each boy gritted his teeth and pushed through the pain, Alexius smiled like a lunatic — the spattering of brown mud shone from his white teeth. He always found the apex of his humor in the darkest places.

Deimos taught us how to work without rest. When he barked commands, our bodies shot to attention. It did not require thinking; it was instinct. We learned this because if one of the boys was slow, or if a boy incorrectly followed a command, our instructor rained fiery hell down upon us. Our bodies learned to stand when our minds were wrought with fatigue. Years later, when we were men, we would sometimes pass beside a training evolution. Even then, after a life of war, something deep inside our muscles would twinge at the command of the barked order.

Iesos taught us how to control the day through focused breathing, which brought us closer to the gods, so he said.

"Feel the air rush from your lungs into the open," he told us. "These actions you may call your own. But, inhale, and know that when the air returns to your body, this is Zeus gifting you life again. So, each breath belongs to him. He instructs Aeolus, keeper of the winds, to keep you alive. It means that Zeus is a part of us. Do not be frightened by this but fortified."

Iesos smiled with a half-dazed look. He was strange, but we loved him.

The instructors each taught us what they knew, and what appeared most important to them.

And some lessons were not learned easily.

But we understood that no matter how dire the day, or how many failures one might encounter while in its clutches, the sun would appear the next morning. Later, it would leave the world in the same manner, and when it did leave, we held hope that the next day might be better. We did not constantly find ourselves in defeat, though that was the only way to learn, but it meant we could envision a future for ourselves in every moment.

Deimos referred to every one of our punishments as "salt." Miss a timing, you received "salt," which meant additional inspections or physical labor. Fail an exercise, or show cowardice in combat, expect "salt." Expect it, as well as an expedition to the sea and back, soaked to your frail bones. For a long time, we never understood why he called it "salt," but eventually we would find out.

The Aegean, in all its glory, provided no mercy to us. It supplied the divine lesson that warriors, in all their exaltation, are inconsequential and small beyond comprehension while battling the forces of nature. Though we became good swimmers, the water pushed against us, and not us against it; we held no physical power over the sea.

We used the cold. We forged our attitudes in its confrontation. We thought we were turning ourselves into animals.

One morning, a Myrmidon arrived carrying a battle-stricken and bloodied helmet to our camp. Broken and slashed across the left cheek, the pieces of twisted steel left charred and blackened marks upon the Myrmidon's hand who carried it. The black plumes of the headpiece were burnt and misshapen. The man approached Teris. He took the helmet under his arm and dropped a knee to the hot sand. I watched my mentor leave, without a word, taking his pain to the far-off mountains. When he returned the next day, his tired eyes appeared glazed, but he addressed us simply, with poise, as he always had.

"Good men fall in the east. Brothers, and sons… and friends. War is hell, and even Myrmidons are susceptible to steel. Do not forget your mortality." With a clang, the old helmet hit the sand in front of us.

I waited for the other boys to disperse to talk to Teris. "Sir," I said.

He turned to me.

"Who do we fight in the east?" I asked.

"A faceless enemy. Whomever our gods and our kings direct us towards," he answered.

"Then your brother," I motioned to the helmet, "his legacy must last forever? Because he stood and died for the gods?"

Teris bowed his head and his lip curled. His head tilted to the side slightly, breaking only for a moment from his role as a hardened leader. "You will find, young man, that the ambitions of rulers always seem to coincidentally align with the will of the gods.

"The gods speak only to them, and give us, those who die, no justification."

"Men often mistake my voice for the one which resides within them," Zeus spoke.

Riddled with dirt and sweat, the soldier's hands shook as he gazed across the smoldering sky.

"Were we tyrants? Were we beasts for taking that which only the gods can give?"

Zeus said nothing. He motioned for the man to continue.

Our days were very structured. We awoke at the same hour together. We dined together. We set our clothes out for inspection, and after that, the churned hills from our daily stampedes awaited us. We spent our evenings cleaning equipment while we sat across from each other. There was conversation, mostly to pass the time, but also to distract us from the overwhelming weight of the road ahead.

Our minds shifted to forget any inklings of just how long we had left. The corridor of torment that lay in front of us was the immediate goal.

Forcibly, we put left in front of right, and right in front of left. And we continued until we finished, which made our lives tolerable, but not easy. All paths must end but they may also last an excrutiatingly long time.

Back to the killing ground we went. This is where we stood our ground against boy and instructor alike, depending on the day, our progression, and the morale of the team. It was a place to assess one's mettle. We only controlled the moments before we stepped inside the crucible of the arena. In those moments, before we had to fight, we used the breathing techniques we'd learned. The cool breeze gently touched our faces, and we soaked up each piece of the surrounding world. Upon our hearts lay the salted mist of the sea. The hard grains of sand etched our skin. In our lungs, the gale flowed freely, sailing through the valleys inside us. We became a part of Greece.

We took these things and forged ourselves within them to steel ourselves against the adversity on the horizon. These dying seconds we adopted to be conscious and to make a firm choice about how we would conduct ourselves once inside the ring. When we crossed the threshold of the ground, however, our three instructors owned us. But by then we entered having envisioned our individual purposes. That made all the difference.

Early in our training, Iesos took us to the outskirts of the camp, between the sea and the endless sky to see the paths and to learn their meanings.

Three trails snaked away from the camp we called home. Iesos had explained these paths to us the first morning we began. He walked along the trail as he spoke, as if he was speaking to the earth and not to us. In odd places, when he spoke the names of the gods, he paused, and for long moments he lost himself as he stared at the clouds.

"The first," he said pointing to the path that led through the green trees and open forest, "is the killing ground, upon which you will prove your strength and ferocity. Call for Kratos when you arrive — let his influence flow through your arms and legs." We watched the mist sway low among the trees and scrape the ground. It rolled over the moss and the roots which jutted out from the earth.

"The second," he motioned to the perilous, rocky route that led to the high mountains, "is where you will prove your worth. Where Gaea guards the ancient path." Above, the clouds moved quickly past the summit of the reaching rock. Like knives, the sharp tips of the mountain loomed high in the heavens.

"Third," he pointed to the desolate, tranquil dirt path that twisted its way along the ocean, "is where you will prove your worthlessness. Phobos shall meet you here, for not all gods are brave." It was the most beautiful of all the trails, nestled between the blue sea and the green hills. We could not see where the snaking line of dirt ended.

Our faces adopted a mixture of confusion and fear, but we tried to steel our gazes and show our determination, as all men must do in the face of choice.

"The third path is the one you will take should you choose to leave. You see this patch of earth, here with the shattered rock. If you quit, you shall take a section of stone with you. May you look upon it forever as a single piece, which should have been part of a formidable whole."

Deimos, who had been silent, stepped forward and pointed to the green grass in front of him.

"Quit, and you will demonstrate your weakness by sticking your sword into the ground, and by leaving your shield hanging upon the handle of the blade. It serves as a reminder to the rest of the battalion that only the strong survive the crucible of training. If you cannot give them honorable death, you will at least leave them hope for death themselves, and you will at least rid them of your softness. It is a poison upon the hearts of warriors. A sickness that drips slowly but corrupts entirely."

Early training had little sense of tactics, but when we needed aggression, we called it forth. We learned anger, and ruthlessness, but also purposefulness and precision. Together we ran the relentless hills surrounding the camp. Each time, we ran with increasing equipment, so that we never became comfortable with the weight we carried. We made an effort to pick up more weight when we were able. And when we picked these things up, we ran past the three trails that left the camp.

In the aftermath of the explanation, and in the following months, countless boys quit, but one in particular stands alone in my memory.

Nikolai was fast. Unbelievably so. Faster than the instructors. His speed over the arduous ground caused havoc. What an attribute to have; speed, Teris had informed us, was the key to all effective warfare. Niko, as we called him, quit. He was not subject to a beating, a failure, or any suffering. It was simply the night, the deafening silence of the tent, which bested him. That evening, enveloped in his own tasks, each boy worked. But Niko... He stood without a word and left. And in the immediate aftermath of his failure, his shoulders and his eyes dropped to the earth.

Ashamed.

Not of himself, but of his inability to push his aching back and legs to carry his brothers across the line. Niko lost because he thought the end was a meager finish line. He failed because there were areas of his training in which he could not rely on his quickness.

Those who remain know that the finish line is false. Those who believe in this line, as Niko did, begin to die immediately upon crossing its threshold.

But his removal from training did not affect the morale of the boys. A new boy would now be the fastest. We used needle and thread to mend the fabric of our team. Together, we continued.

The solemn gaze of Nikolai, as he placed his armor on the hill, was now burned into memory. We could only imagine the personal toll it took upon him, and that sentiment lingered at first. But the hillside was soon littered with the lasting legacy of other failures. The ominous graves of willpower sat as the spray from the ocean met the rusting metal. Beads of ocean water lingered upon forgotten steel — catacombs of the soul atop Grecian soil.

We who lasted and who cauterized our wounds, we endured. The sun rose with us, and though our lives were difficult, we also knew contrast. We did not seek, and we enjoyed the smallest of things that the world granted to us.

At the same time, we did not accept that we were all exactly the same. In becoming a proficient and ruthless team, we understood that our personalities clashed at times. Our convictions were not identical, but the fact that we could accept each other meant that when we brought death upon our enemies, we did so because we were each a piece of the men we fought against. Finding strength meant accepting that not all of us were the same, and that we often had more similarities with our enemies than our friends. Deimos spoke to us of this issue.

Deimos was harsh with his words. They stung the truth of a wasp's needle. "To learn a man must be able to listen. He need not accept, but he must understand that which he does not believe. Only then will this team begin to succeed. Until then, we will break you and your effectiveness into pieces to feed to the vultures."

Each morning, the light emerged above the dead and each evening it disappeared over the sea, far away from the crypts of our former compatriots. Every day the earth underwent the same routine, and yet the memories of those who quit lay still in our minds and on the hillside.

We watched as some of the best of us walked the solitary ocean path. Their equipment added to the pile. It looked so heavy on their shoulders but sat so light upon the ground.

By midsummer, only about a third of our original group had stayed in place and thrived. We would awake each morning to find we were still alive, and we were grateful for it. No boy who left attempted to recover their armor or restart their training. The threaded fabric left no room for them. Our team reserved no gaps. We accepted only victors.

But we did not pretend our success was completely our own. All men must trust in their friends over themselves.

Some men are never confronted with this idea. Some warriors awaken in the morning as if it were a certainty. They do not pursue, nor do they risk their trust in a bond with others. They exist as lost vessels. And when they die, they die surrounded by people and yet, alone.

The mentors never harassed us once they deemed the day over. Not once was that promise broken. When they parted, raucous laughter and recounts of the day were common.

But once those sentiments died down for the night, it was silent.

Silence was the greatest enemy we ever faced. It was easy to be courageous in the violent symphony of the sword, or when aggression ran rampant in the hallowed ground of our combative training. But it was the suffering silence that was the true killer. It was the shaking in one's hands, the buildup of self-doubt in the quiet stillness and the vastness of one's mind, that conquered all.

Silence could break even the strongest boy if it was not destroyed immediately. A treacherous immobility was sometimes, illogically, a consequence of talent, and a consequence of ease, for when a boy has no necessity to struggle, he is then left with his own disloyal thoughts. And since his mind knows all his weaknesses and doubts, it holds a tactical advantage over his attitude. It can convince the boy to abdicate himself from struggle. This is only possible if the boy does not possess self-realization. This is only true if he does not practice the internal ability to engage in self-combat. Iesos taught us this.

The softest spoken of the three instructors brought us through the mountain pass to a still lake. Every boy sat and stared at their reflections. He showed us the fundamental and crucial difference between stillness and silence.

"I present to you, young warriors, the only man you must prove yourself to. Do not fall victim to that which became the demise of Narcissus, but rather look deeper. It is too easy to come to terms with one's character and decisions in the fires of war, when the arrows shriek and the swords ring, but here, at the pond, is where you shall return when the music ceases. Too many pieces of the earth shine a reflection back to the man — a sea, a pond, a finished blade of metal — and so a warrior must be comfortable with staring at himself."

The lake was the first time I ever had to engage with the demon inside me.

Achilles and I rarely sat still, because our talent lacked. Even when his tasks remained unfinished, he still offered to help with mine. I watched as he helped lace my gear — the task I loathed. The talented ones had finished their tasks. Ours were not even close to being done. Because we still folded, sharpened, and organized, and because we had no chance of perfection on the first try, we never found ourselves thinking too deeply. In the most paradoxical of ways, our imperfections were our saviors, our ineptness, our luck.

Achilles' hands were soft and deft. No anger or aggression flew from his movements. When I was young, I thought his gentleness was a detriment, but later I realized the world needs all kinds of people. As I watched him, I heard a small chirping coming from his cot.

"What is that?" I asked.

"Please, don't tell them," he answered.

He pulled a box from underneath his cot. In it sat a small bird, no bigger than a fist. Its feathers were lined at the top with a deep blue, though they faded into white near the bottom. The swallow had a beautiful yellow beak and bright eyes. The right wing was crippled. Pieces of Achilles' rations littered the box. Achilles had been caring for it for a few days.

"I stumbled across him on the mountain. Vultures pecked at the mother. I could not leave him there to die…" He quickly put the box away as another boy approached.

The next night, we took the bird to the ocean to breathe the fresh air. The boy with the blonde hair revealed to me a small fragment of his youth.

"I do not know my father, like you. It is not unlike countless boys in my village… None of them made it out before the mercenaries arrived and destroyed our village, only I. The soldiers for hire took everything we ever had, back when I was happy, when I could still see the smile of my mother before they murdered her. Everything I was and had is gone now, and yet it still haunts me, long into the night."

Self-destruction is only combatted by movement.

In the brutal moments of exercise, when the body is at its absolute limit, where the muscles flex, and the blood rushes through the veins, thoughts concentrate on the relief that might wash over a boy, if only he would quit. But we understood life beyond that point. We understood that to let go and fall to the ground, to fall victim to the temptation of subsiding pain meant to fail not only in the moment, but in life — that was where we found our purpose. We pushed back against what we externally felt. Succeeding meant not only continuing each day but finding new avenues to survive. In each of our darkest moments, we succeeded because we knew the next hour would come, the next minute would find us, and the next enduring second would take us away with the tide. But, as in all things, we needed to navigate those seconds with real intent, and innovation.

Deimos screamed profanities in our faces, but he never struck our bodies, only our shields. He did not engage in some game of chance, because he knew the mental consequences of what might happen to us should we fall victim to the easy road of blaming the unfair things in life. Instead, he spoke with devastating brashness, which is far more useful.

I remember him once, in the month of Poseidon, when the winter surged, when the air became crisp, and the steam took shape in the air radiating from our pulsing chests. I was in the forefront of the group, grinding myself into dust on the mountain, but leading by example. He ran with me for the better part of the day, saying little, but knowing that I could hear his armor, which was far heavier than mine, clanging against his body. As we rounded the turn we called "Wolfbane," which looks southward towards the Aegean, he turned to me. Not once had he ever spoken to me with the care he showed in this moment. For an instant it frightened me. But his words rang with courage.

"Momentum favors the warrior. All warfare is based on speed and aggression. But to deny one's own arrogance is to create death. We run towards the hills, not away from them. We run towards them because they humble us. Because when we fly down them, transformed and transfixed, diving like hawks towards prey, we slam our enemies with a potency such as they have never seen before. Take the highest path and you will find yourself at the end, surrounded by enemies but calm like Lycaon under the harvest moon. You will understand in that moment that you have the tactical prowess and advantage over them. You have done well, but the road always continues."

"And if we make the right choice, we will last the battle?" I asked.

"I speak not of war."

He took off up the path. His pace was one I could not match, nor fathom to.

If we did not yield, and if we listened to the imperceptible force that drove us on, we might win the true war.

Though the hard days in the ring were numerous, there were also other days we found uplifting. The first time I perfected a combination attack against my peer, I saw what might have been a glint of pride in Teris' eye. There was a great unity in my body. My sword, now light through my strengthened shoulders, soared through the air, cutting the whining wind with ease.

Ducking the broad swing of my opponent, I twisted my shield parallel to the sand to glance the blow. I swiveled towards the back of my opponent.

The sand hardened beneath my flexed toes and I made it there before his turn. I thought later about the floating pebbles and about the will of the earth itself. I felt in this moment as if I were one with the beach. I felt much more than a single boy, playing at war. And when the earth pushed back against my feet, it was a response to true and clear intent. Fused with spirit and earth, my grip tightened. It was a clear force, but one I did not fully understand at the time.

Had this been war, I could have slashed the neck above the iron collar guard of this man, and I would finally have earned the blood on my black armor. But it wasn't war. It was training, and in training, there are only two outcomes. When one of us found victory, another had to lose. At the same time that I was propelling myself forward, I was sacrificing the progress of another. The only way we balanced these losses was by learning and extracting the true lesson from the battle. Training is nothing but the ability to learn from loss, while to lose in war is peril.

War is far more brutal in how it blackens the souls of men. We would come to learn this.

Though the skies emerged each morning, some skies billowed darker than others. Fog hindered the sunrise one morning when Achilles and I squared for combat. We circled each other. We stood to the test. Which boy had the mettle to make the first dash?

I made an overhead attempt and rang my steel blade off the top of Achilles' shield. As he parried my attempt, I flew left, and wrapped his shoulder with my left arm, isolating the right arm joint in which he held his sword. The weapon was now useless. I cranked the joint past the point of straightening, and with a heavy downwards blow I knocked his sword to the dust. Fear consumed his eyes. He stumbled backwards into the dirt, protected only by his shield. I swung. Achilles blocked, but he scrambled across the dirt as I repeatedly and ruthlessly echoed my blade on his shield — his only weapon. He did not search for his blade. He continued to block and to whimper with terror. I could do nothing but let the boy return to his feet. Achilles stood, but he had suffered a crushing defeat. I looked at the instructors with an expression of confusion for what to do next.

Deimos had seen enough.

The type of surrender that had gripped Achilles in that moment was a despicable action. It constituted a reprisal from Deimos, who sent him flying to the ground. Achilles' shield cracked as if it had suffered the kick of a bucking black stallion.

"You plan to fight this man with only a shield!? What, will you pray his arms tire, and his legs give? Pathetic. I do not care if you die on the field of battle. But die acting heroically! You will, if you continue to act in such a cowardly manner, never touch the fields of Elysium, boy."

That night we sat beside the murky ocean. We had continued another day. We took these moments for ourselves, and to think about nothing at all except to be present in the small victories. The endless sky sat above us, angry with the charges of thunder. It ripped across the sea as the currents of electric light ran through the clouds.

"I thought then that you, Zeus, may be watching over us.'

Zeus spoke, *"Where you find the thunder, you shall also find me."*

Reminiscing, the warrior remembered how the anger of the skies had torn through him yet always gave him the strength to continue.

"In our hearts we felt the same."

There was something within us, in these times, that made us feel part of the earth. We had iron in our veins and salt in our wounds, like the great terrain that surrounded us. We were, in these moments, part of the wrath of the world, but we held the tempest in our hands.

We noticed that as we grew, we mastered our skills, and then we were then given the next weapon. This in turn required more strength and more tactical prowess — this gave us increasing responsibility. The shortsword is light, but it has limits of reach and power. We traded it in for an iron-plated broadsword. Not only did we master these weapons, but our physical strength seemed to rise to the requirement. Instead of dropping due to fatigue, we rallied. This was almost impossible to understand, as our bodies had never adapted so quickly to something so difficult before. The heavier the weapon, the more adaptation, and the more responsibility we shouldered. We progressed in unison. We weren't men yet, but we made our way towards it, and we climbed the steep slope to purpose. Through our incessant suffering our souls shined bright. And when we picked up the heaviest thing we could, we found ourselves happy to remain another day.

In the middle of our tent, Deimos set a single black shield.

Suspended upon a wood stand, it gleamed in the moonlight. In the daytime, we pulled the canvas open, and the shield stole the light from the sun. It radiated no reflection onto our ground. It showed record of its past. There were no horses, no depictions of warriors, or desperate calls to the pantheon upon the shield; it only bore the same scars as the men. The Myrmidons did not seek the help of others, even the gods. They did not rely on the proficiency of others to live.

Zeus interrupted, *"Why do the Myrmidons not seek our godly help for victory as other soldiers do? Do they consider themselves apart or above pious acts?"*

"With respect, Zeus, Myrmidons revere the gods, but they do not rely on them. Though I admit I thought the same as you at first. When I asked Iesos about that very fact, he addressed me with a far more serious tone than he ever had before.

"'How many gods have you squared with at the killing ground, young man? We hold them in the highest degree of esteem. We pray. We are borne from them. We, in turn, respect them so deeply we do not plea to them for favors or solicit them for strength. We validate the power they gave to us as our piety. Our souls burn with theirs.'"

Zeus nodded. *"Continue. The shield sits even now upon the stand. Though I regret that the dust collects upon its edges at this moment. The flaps of the tent wave, unkept, in the Greek breeze, straying from the sea."*

"That pains me to hear, Zeus."

"The world has changed much since your ascent. Time is no friend to a heroic life."

Beds lined the centerpiece of the tent. Each night I stared deep into its dark chasms. Each morning I awoke to its symbol. No boy was to touch it, accidentally, nor move it purposely for convenience.

Our weapons became deadlier, and our tactics became more complex. Our clothes and our organized gear remained as steadfast as the shield. When we awoke in the morning, we finished the tasks we needed to, when the shield shone brightest. In the long night, when it seemed darkest to us, we finished them all the same.

"Should we not harness the power of the sun? Instead, our armor shines in the night," I asked Iesos.

Iesos responded, "Our power comes from our recognition and integration of that which we cannot see, but also that which we cannot understand. To walk by faith is to walk the path of a Myrmidon. The gods guide us when our eyes fail."

As the days and the weeks passed, we hardly noticed the change of the seasons, nor did we feel them. Our bodies and our minds turned to stone with the excessive shifting of the world. We had no time for such trivial things as temperature, comfort, and happiness. There was too much to do, too much to learn.

One quiet morning, Teris sat us down at the firepit as the sun began to rise on the horizon. He spoke with authority, and his voice carried the smoke across the waves.

"How can a man avoid the evil inside him?"

A boy, fair-skinned with mahogany brown eyes answered.

Leandros. Lion man.

"We cannot be evil; our cause is that of protection against evil. We fight for Greece, and not for ourselves."

His answer was calm and collected.

But Teris shook his head.

"Admirable as that might be, the truth is murkier. The most dangerous man is the one who believes himself to be good, for he has not the ability to combat his downfalls. You are human, and so, you also have those fracture lines of the heart which we all do. These cracks, you have seen them; they are the ones in the earth where the smoke escapes and rises into the air. In your souls, these cracks allow the evil to seep through. We live our lives in the service of something more, of the creed of brotherhood, and in the pursuit of bravery for each other.

"We search for transcendence, of the soul and of the mind, but we lose it as quickly as we find it. Thus, every action we take, no matter how trivial it may seem, is like a rock cast upon a still pond. It ripples and destroys men. We recognize malevolence, and so we are certain that we aren't conducting deeds of that nature. Through suffering in peace, we suffer far less in life."

Zeus spoke, *"All warriors, regardless of which army they fight for or which*

campaign they perish in, or which beach they die upon, always believe their side to be the correct one."

"We believed a similar tale, because others had told it to us." Shaking his head in embarrassment, the Myrmidon flinched with the sting of regret.

Teris continued as we listened. "Only men who cultivate violent abilities stand toe to toe with violence. To be peaceful only means that a warrior makes himself susceptible to anyone who declares themselves foe. But you must avoid…" he scanned the group with his outstretched hand, halting as he met the gaze of Pyrros, "…the urge to always be violent. This is yet another way to burn that which you have built. Only bring forth this violence when needed. Act ruthless, only when the world requires you to do so."

But he lost our gaze and turned his head towards the tall grass. As he sliced his hand along the swaying meadow, I was certain I saw agony within him. It took hold of me for a moment, to see this giant of a man, in stature and attitude, withholding some untold hurt. It humanized him. But as the gallant cries of enthusiasm erupted from the group, my doubts disappeared. The vigor of the boys I would now call my brothers took me over, and my understanding of him drifted away.

The speech roused us, and as we completed our tasks for the day, we did so with a renewed sense of purpose. Through the hard running, the savage fighting, and the endless lessons, we held our heads high and wore our armor with ease.

Teris joked with us when there were no other instructors around. We respected him just as much as the others, but we loved listening to his stories; we were equals in those moments. Sitting in the sunshine, we ate and drank, and he told stories. When soldiers tell stories to one another, they are full of humor, much more than sadness.

"Your only talent cannot be killing," he joked. "What women will you attract acting only as brutes?" His comment was in jest, but, as always, it rang heavy with truth. Teris spoke the least. He did not fire his words with the passion of Deimos, nor veil them with the piety of Iesos. It is astounding how important this simplicity is, and how so few men possess the ability to convey it with any conviction.

That was an easy day, in an otherwise difficult life.

Though one day may be easy, the night can still consume. That night, the anger of the gods hid the moon from us. The sea raged and the wind tore through the quiet camp, ringing across the steel and black armor. My dreams were helpless and cruel. Sweat beaded from my forehead like spring rain. The wind was mild, though my temperature flared. I exited our tent countless times to submerge my head in the cold ocean. I hoped and prayed that this fever might leave me. I did not sleep. My body felt weak. My once strong legs could not lift my now much larger frame from the cot. When the unrelenting sun began to break, I knew what hardships lay ahead.

And that day was not a day to be weak, to falter. Loaded with gear, we had to run the mountain. I could not lag behind given my already lacking talent.

"The war will happen," Deimos barked at us, "no matter what the day, no matter what the weather, no matter how willing or unwilling a warrior is to fight. Be prepared. Combat is preceded by the conflict within. If you cannot win against yourself, you are sure to die a gruesome death at the hand of a man that can."

I hesitate to express to you my weakness, Zeus, god of gods, but the next hours of my life became a blur. As we ran, the heat from the sun cascaded upon the rocks. It burned us and reflected from the sea, drying the dirt, and scorching our feet. Some fever took hold of me, in body and mind. In fact, they were two fiends in consort. My negative thoughts fed on the sickness that gripped my body.

As I rounded a corner, near the peak of the mountain, my vision had narrowed itself to the size of a pinpoint. I could see nothing and hear nothing. I had only the smallest focus in my gaze. My breathing was shallow, and hoarse, and I felt the blood rising in my head.

My destructive thoughts took hold.

Not in this moment, please, not here of all places, I thought. *Let me at least die in battle with my brothers.* I cared not whether my death would arrive after decades of conflict; I could die with the first swing of the first enemy sword that I met. That would be a heroic death. Not here, with no image of a heroic finality in my sight.

The last thing I heard was the tide of the Aegean crashing into the shore far below.

When I came to, I saw myself, floating above the sand.

I had pictured a more sublime death, but I was not granted the immortality I craved. At least I would not perish unaccompanied. One of my brothers would eventually stumble across me. They would burn me on the pyre, tell stories about me, laugh, and Alexius would supply tales of wit and charm that would otherwise, without him, be unamusing and dull. At least I would not be forsaken to the island that had broken me. The breeze would take my scattered remains — I could be a part of all Greece.

I opened my eyes to meet the Fortunate Isles of the west, where all Greek warriors find themselves in time. I realized then that I was still drifting upon the mountain path. In fact, I had not perished at all. The clouds swayed in the Greek sky above as I rose to my feet. I could look up, and so I could get up, and remain.

Rising to my feet, it seemed that all that had changed in me was the decision I'd made in a moment of agonizing pain. Either I would die in the sand, or my willpower would stand firm to the test put before me — a simple thing, and hard, like life. We forget who pulls the reigns of life — the body or the mind. Does the stallion choose the path, or the rider? Does the steed run into the wilderness of spearheads, or does the warrior?

All I had to do was quiet a momentary voice, a calling siren from a distant shore. All that I had to do was not give in to the lies I told myself.

The hours passed and I remember nothing. My feet moved as if in a trance, but they moved forward and so that was all that mattered. I would make it. It was now an inevitability.

Finally arriving back in camp, I threw my body in the shallow of the ocean to cool down my overheated body. Alexius sat beside me, lost in his own vision.

"Surprised those chicken legs carried you up and down the hill," he said, smirking, but wrought with fatigue. I said nothing, but as I lay on my back in the ocean and stared towards the heavens, I smiled. We sat together as the waves crashed against the shore, flowing across my abdomen to the crest of my head. The ocean breathed its waves against us, and together we sat inside the lungs of the sea.

"Do you ever worry, my friend," Alexius added, his elbow buried in the sand and his body facing me, "that we spend far more time training to run than to fight?" He smiled.

When I could finally stand, I saw Achilles cross the finish. The sweat, the dirt, and the redness in the whites of his eyes showed weakness in him, but determination as well. His blonde hair was black with dust. He walked past us and sat down in the shallows of the ocean, as I had. His breathing was labored, and blood poured from a wound on his leg. Bandaging his ailment, tears fell from his eyes to the sea. Salt to salt.

It wasn't war. It was how we prepared our minds for the brutality of what was to come.

But Achilles looked beyond broken.

Yes, Achilles, the same. The warrior of history. And far before that the leader of our tribe. We heard fables of his origin, but back then I never saw such things in him. It was, in fact, his human roots, his downfalls, and his ability to overcome them, that became the catalysts for his heroism. Though, how we define heroism may be our biggest point of contention, Zeus.

For these reasons, humanity becomes a hazard for potential downfall as well. You see, in all men, there exists at all times both love and hate, courage and cowardice — the great dichotomy. We walked the line, but some men fell further than others by nature of their position.

In our eyes we saw not who we used to be, but what we had the potential for, and we learned to look at all men in the same way. We did not understand at that time that we also needed to be wary of the potential for self-destruction in all men, even the heroic.

I stood as Iesos and Teris approached, still catching my breath, my chest heaving with pain. Our priest spoke to us.

"You were decisive in matters which might have otherwise compromised your character. You took dominion over yourself. Fidelity and devotion to the gods above all. Destiny, above past," said Iesos. He was speaking to us, but his gaze remained fixed on the sea.

He continued as we breathed heavily.

"When a man first experiences hardship, or the threat of a viable challenge, he should do so in the confines of his training, or under the watch of his mentors. But not in the grips of battle with a capable enemy. He will only know this when his body fills with steel, and the light of his life leave his eyes. He will, in those moments, reflect on all of that which he did wrong. Some of the actions he took in life were gallant and honorable. These might appear in the tales of old men. But the warrior will know the truth in death. He will only regret that which he did not have the courage to carry out. But courage has not failed you here today."

Teris smiled at Achilles. "Well done." He ruffled the blonde hair of Achilles as he walked away.

I found myself admiring Achilles in that moment, not in the way we all admired Pyrros, but for something else. It was something I could not quite articulate at the time, and that I could not understand. I did not yet understand myself well enough, and so I would not attempt to understand him. And besides, I was, until recently, lying half-dead in the ocean. My primary focus was to get myself together, one piece at a time. I had destroyed myself in the furnace of the pursuit, and I needed to now repair the metal.

The rest of the days I suffered through but survived. Achilles suffered far greater than any of us. By this time in our development, we had an easy time of learning drilled movements at the square, cleaning our weapons with the cloths and oil provided, sharpening our swords with the smooth stones given to us, running the high peaks each day, and submerging ourselves in the cold of the ocean. But Achilles still struggled.

The sea was a great equalizer. Untamable, but acceptable with the right endurance.

In winter, I enveloped myself in the ocean; the shockwave sucked all the breath from my body. No matter how many times I forced myself into the waves, the frigid water chiseled away at my will. Achilles might have been the only boy who had a worse time than I. When we assessed ourselves against the might of the cold, he shook, his lips would turn blue, and the tears poured from his eyes, undistinguishable from the brine. But we all went in just the same, and we went in together, because no boy would dare to be the single one left standing on the comfortable warm sand.

But it was not the cold that ground us down. It was the salt. The Myrmidons, having gone through the same hardships that we now faced, knew that the salt, once it made its way to the dark corners of both the physical body and of the mind, would dry, stick to our bodies, rub, and grind as we ran, and then in our wounds the salt would make its way to our blood like leeches and burn like acid. That is what made it worse. A warrior can weather brief suffering, but the slow wearing away of one's soul can break almost anyone. We performed no drills, nor exercises in the ocean, for that would warm our blood and in turn create the opposite effect of the goal. And yet, we found that when we did immerse ourselves in the salt water, our wounds healed. We sat, freezing, with the water at our necks, and listened to the muffled tides.

When the skin healed, we would again face the crucible of the sea and the salt would find those places again. We had to accept the pain once more, and in the places most scarred by our salt we had to become tougher.

Soon, the salt of the ocean became our sweat, and this became our power against the minor failings of our self-restraint. We understood then why even the smallest of infractions was rewarded with "salt." We did not need further clarification; the ocean had made its point. Mastering our bodies and the fear of the cold, we used it to make us fiercer, and more deadly.

Our training consisted of many brutalities. We stripped the trees from the forest with two-handed iron cleavers, prying loose the old bark glued to each core. We carried the smooth giants. Their resting places were arbitrary to us, but Teris would often note, "Not all plans should be clear to the warrior. In time the pieces shall fit together." And the next morning we carried the logs back to the killing ground. When we ran the same trail upon which we had carried the logs, we saw that the loose ground had hardened like plaster under our feet. The earth, content with our grit, had presented to us a gift — our bodies now flew up the hill.

We used our physiques as our weights. Soon, they loaded our bodies with more war gear during exercise. We needed to be sharp like the edges of our swords, and steadfast like the wood that lined our shields. This combination created unity. On the larger scale it created a battalion of one man, grasping one sword and shield, armed with the strength of a hundred

No warrior is afraid of numerical disadvantage, but he may lay awake in his bed at night thinking about the one ferocious man — the impenetrable warrior who might finally kill him. We strived to not become a group of warriors but rather one entity. We transformed the one man into many. Sewn together by the unity of our bodies, we carried our weapons. And so, at the end of all things, every one of us became the nightmare of ordinary men.

"But no man sits atop the pillar of fear, no god, even. Each of us is afraid of something. We all have titans we lock away in the deep, dark crevasses of our thoughts. So, Myrmidon, did you act with a complete absence of fear? Were the Myrmidons truly so powerful?"

"No, Zeus, we acted in spite of such things. We died in war. Other men bested us in combat. We wore armor in the hopes it would protect us. We believed deep down that could defeat all enemies. But every warrior, no matter how powerful, is still a slave to his own nightmares."

One morning, after the sea had made its way into the recesses of our limbs, our legs ached from running across the loose sand. Our organized gear sat in the corner of the tent. Ready for the challenges of the day, we sat and watched the sun rise from the beach — it was one of the only reprieves we received from the constant assault of the instruction. We took the small beauties the world offered us. We ached; we lived. Each boy watched, and each one found himself looking into both the ocean and his heart. We used this time to try to understand our faults, and our strengths. While each boy did this alone, it was not isolating. Solitude and solidarity consumed the deafening silence, broken only by the crashing waves.

As the beach began to warm in the sunshine, we left to follow Teris to an unknown task. Following without asking was the norm. Our bodies moved without question — we took the steps we needed to with the faith that they would be the right ones. As we walked down the shoreline, we found ourselves sitting before a granite wall that peaked about thirty feet above our heads. Teris, without speaking to us, scaled the wall with ease. The movements of his hands and his feet were powerful, but they flowed like water. It was not the strength in his arms that propelled him up, but rather the fearlessness with which he moved. A current ran through his body that directed the precision of his choices.

In a final movement he disappeared over the top, and, leaning over the edge, motioned for us to follow.

The wall itself was not imposing, but as we gripped the small imperfections in the stone, we realized how difficult it would be to follow him. Knowing we would not be able to replicate with ease the route he took, we began. As we climbed, we tried to remove the fear from our minds, the fear of the fall. Our hands slipped upon the glasslike surface of the stone, and along our fingertips the friction from our minor mistakes burned and ripped the skin from its place. We were not artists as he was, but we muscled and grit our teeth and forced our bodies through the ordeal, which all men must do and not only upon the wall.

It grounded us in the moment. We had to make each movement purposeful and accurate. The climb required nothing less than our absolute focus, so that the rest of our suffering, the bleeding pieces of skin on our hands, drifted away.

We climbed higher; the wall demanded more focus. The higher we climbed, the more our world shrank. Nothing else mattered in the instant, for we could only control our bodies. There were no politics, no tyrants, no farms, no labor, no theft of youth, no rage of the sea, no downfalls of men. We controlled our lives completely in our hands and feet, and nothing more. It was strange to feel so insignificant, and yet to control something so important.

As I neared the top of the pitch and looked down, I realized in that moment that the climb was not an epic mountain, nor a grand wall of godly proportions searching for the clouds above. It was small, and inconsequential. The wall itself meant nothing to the landscape of the earth — a tiny imperfection on the land such as our fingers had found on the rock itself. But despite that, a fall from here would ravage my body and shatter my bones and limbs. That made it imperative that I keep moving. My hands shook with fear, which was slowly creeping its way through the veins in my legs and spreading its disease to my heart. I stopped. Frozen, like ice in the Grecian sun. Alexius appeared beside me.

"The world would be better off without you," he laughed, "but it will be my job to pull your corpse from the sand, so I implore you not to jump. Though, it would also save me having to help you complete your tasks each night, so, in truth, just go for it. See if you can fly like the Aetos Dios." He grinned.

"This boy..." Zeus said. *"His heart is light, and for that I envy him."*

"He always had something to say, even in peril," the Myrmidon responded, but turned his eyes from Zeus' gaze.

I couldn't help but smile as I stood frozen on the wall, and in an instant the fear drained from the arteries of my dread. I was only frightened because I had stopped moving. If I had continued with the same fervor, I would have been able to avoid those friendly jests thrown at me by Alexius. But I had to admire him, for he did not enjoy heights either, as he'd told me this long before the climb. He was able to use those gifts given to him by the gods and make light of what might otherwise be brutal.

In the days that followed, as I reflected on the wall, I had trouble finding what exactly resided in me that was similar to the unique quality he had. It seemed to me that even in the smallest of pursuits, rooted in the slightest hills we climbed, there was always the risk of the fall. So, we had to force ourselves in life to function as if presented with two options: to climb, or to acquiesce to the pressure. As in all things, the hardest traverse was to come just before the end; the darkest time of the night lay just before dawn. By overcoming the top of the rock, we could find the world horizontal once more. We could only trust our instincts and our grit and have faith. Maybe my power was faith.

Men cannot know what lies above, and so they must reach their arm over the precipice, unsure of what they might grasp, but with the hope that a hold presents itself. At that moment everything relies on the commitment of the body to throw itself into the unknown abyss. We found the weightlessness we craved, and the nothingness in-between. The Myrmidons spoke of such hallowed words. It was courage.

As we completed the climb and caught up to our mentor, he motioned us to rest. Sitting in the lush of the green field that lay beyond the climb, he spoke to us. Warm wind blew through the tall reeds and comforted our battered bodies. It was a gentle reminder of the beauty in the world despite its harshness. The calmness of the valley soothed us.

"War is exhausting," Teris told us. "The true confrontation comes while under a secondary siege of combat. At the moment when the thrill of the fight subsides, your arms and legs become a burden and your reactions dim. You must remain sharp. The Myrmidons train for the second wave of battle. This is where men die."

We sat for a while in the summer breeze until our hearts became still. The lesson of the day imprinted upon us. We made our way to the beach again.

On our beach sat four stones, each of which we would need to lift from the ground to the shoulder before becoming Myrmidons. Our black armor awaited, but our other trials loomed heavy. Some of the boys looked curious. In a playful manner, and much too early in our training, they decided to attempt to lift the heaviest one.

This rock was a true beast — a piece that'd crumbled from the mountain above. A great splinter of the rigid earth, it was as large as a Myrmidon's black shield. Jagged at the corners, the rock required the strength of the back, but also a complete steeling of the mind. The edges stole the blood from the creases of our fingers. The stone, when dropped, would force the grains of sand apart and in turn wedge itself deeper into the sand. The boy who failed was to blame for the difficulty of the next attempt. A failure was detrimental to the group, for pointless efforts.

Only when one felt ready should they attempt the lift, or they must live with the knowledge that they negatively affected the lives of their brothers in arms. Despite my wretched strength, I managed to budge the rock, near the ankle line, before it slammed onto the top of my right foot. I learned a rapid and painful lesson.

Pyrros saw us attempting this rock. He became angrier and angrier as our weak arms flexed in the hot sun. His rage finally flared when Achilles failed to move the stone whatsoever. In a flash, he was on us, his fury propelling his gigantic arms towards the stones. His broad shoulders shoved me to the side, and I stumbled over a group of logs that had washed onto the shore and fell. I watched as Pyrros enclosed his fingers around the knifelike edges of the heaviest stone, and with a great yell he lifted it with ease. His eyes met mine, and I thought for a moment he desperately wanted to crush me with the stone. He looked at me with a lust for death. Fear gripped me.

But before he could execute, Iesos appeared from behind the cliff and motioned for him to stop. Pyrros did, but I would not forget his face and his unexplainable rage until my final days with him.

With great difficulty we did lift the stones. There is no story here, Zeus, the trial was difficult and simple, as our lives must be. As a result of our hardships and pain, our bodies adapted, again, only as a consequence of our vigorous work, and not of our talents.

The morning after, the sun shining from Nikolai's lonely armor glistened and lit the dew-covered grass. From afar the image seemed not of this world. The hill sparkled and moved with the weather, and once more, we were summoned to the killing fields.

Beckoned to the proving grounds of our aggression and anger, Pyrros and Achilles squared off first. We worried for the blonde boy. We worried about any of our group who had to battle the anger and physicality of Pyrros. Even though we knew that death was improbable, we shifted our feet upon the ground as we stood in waiting. As the battle ensued, the rest of the boys lined the grounds and cheered on their comrades.

It was clear who the dominating force was. As Pyrros parried Achilles' desperate efforts with ease, I watched as the faces of the spectators turned from aggression to fright. My stomach turned to knots as I watched the unfolding horror. Why did I not act? I knew Pyrros would destroy the young boy, and yet somehow, in some dark corner of myself, I wanted to see the violence.

Achilles made attempts at catching Pyrros on the flank, but the stronger boy predicted each movement. With each failed effort, Achilles lost more and more momentum. As Achilles dove to the left, Pyrros anticipated this move, deftly sidestepped the blow, and slammed the edge of his shield into the back of Achilles' neck with a deafening crack. I looked to the skies. I heard you above, Zeus, but found a clear, sunny day.

He hit the ground with such force that pebbles shot upwards into the air. They appeared to me as if they lingered, the blood seeping from the body of Achilles to saturate the earth. The rocks only returned to their place when Pyrros began to step forward. The instructors watched the pebbles too. The three mentors looked at one another, impressed with the show, yet displaying no signs of approval. When Achilles failed to rise, Deimos interrupted his suffering.

"Get up, boy!" he said, in his voice of embers.

We were not addressed by our names at any point, only by "boy."

As Achilles attempted to rise from the earth, Pyrros slammed his back with the broadside of his bronze shield and sent the blonde boy back into the ground. His usual shining hair was brown with the pasty mix of earth and blood. He did not move.

We watched as his labored breathing caused slight rises in his chest. *He may be dying now*, we thought.

"Pathetic." A gruff voice broke the silence.

Deimos looked disgusted with the faintness of Achilles. His performance had been meek, yes, but I was certain that if I got hit with that much force, I would have died a coward's death. It is far easier to watch and to judge than to endure judgement yourself.

The beaten face of Achilles hung lifeless as we carried him over our shoulders. Blood flowed down his shirtless torso, finding its own path of least resistance, in streams. In his right hand his shield remained lashed to his wrist, and he gripped the handle, though it pained him greatly to do so. Hypatios and I brought him to the healers.

Deimos, still furious, yelled as we departed the ground, "Pay careful attention! Look into his eyes, boys. On a distant battlefield this would have ended with death! For you and him. Tighten him up or die with him."

The next day, Achilles could not move. His sheets hung heavy with blood. The breeze blew through the canvas tent as we left him to heal. Visibly shaken, we took our places as usual, ready for the day's instruction. But something was wrong. There were no quips, no whispers, no jokes. Suddenly it had all become real. The consequences became something more than "salt."

Teris began. The instructors knew that our spirits shook with fear that morning. "When a warrior's gaze breaks, does his body falter also? Can a man continue fighting long after he crosses the line, at the peak of the tempest? What actions should he take when the naivety of his youth shatters like broken steel in the forge?"

He walked the line of exhausted boys as we listened to him. He stopped in front of me and rapped my bare chest sharply with the edge of his closed fist. He scanned the group.

"Can he retain his grit, and still continue to use the wisdom he has collected from the years of his life? Or will he crumble under the immensity of the moment? Will he forget that to move is to live, to halt is to die? Could it be that we might solve these philosophies, which have haunted men and thinkers throughout the centuries through simple, physical combat? Let us expose all lies and reveal all courage. Let us find a light in the darkest place." His eyes locked upon mine. "What will you follow, young man?"

"My heart," I responded.

"Your heart," he repeated, nodding his head in agreement. "The heart of a soldier."

Achilles took weeks to recover. He survived, but he needed to rest. During the most silent moments, while the rest of us fought, ran, swore, and trained like animals, he healed. Pyrros never went to see the blonde boy. Twice their fleeting eyes met from the crack in the open tent, but the victor showed no remorse. Achilles then had to contend with the look of his destroyer for the rest of the soundless day. But he did not quit. He engaged in a different battle than us. Something changed in him when he exited the tent, still limping. Where I knew a boy of compassion and meekness, out stepped a warrior full of anger and hate.

While his body healed, his mind altered. He still struggled in the months to come, but there was a renewed attitude of vengeance within him. A hate which I had never before seen in him planted a small seed deep within the fertile earth of his heart.

On the beach I stumbled across the body of the swallow Achilles had adopted. Rolling up and down the beach with the tides, green sea foam and brine covered its once beautiful body. Its beak was open. It had succumbed to its injuries. With sorrow, I realized that Achilles had been too injured himself to feed it, and that I had done nothing to help him, having been too focused on my own trials.

I hated myself for being so blind and selfish.

And the end of training grew near.

We awoke far before the sun to the sound of metal swords clattering against strong shields. The three mentors we had come to know so well cascaded into our tent and began screaming and shouting at us to don our gear. There was an unscheduled test to be had today — that could be the only explanation of this. We steeled our eyes and forced our skin to bond to the frosty morning metal of our plates and our shields, which was worse the earlier the hour. But as we passed the black shield that sat in the center of our tent, we slammed the handles of our swords into our chests.

Leandros spoke up as we exited the tent, our hands shaking with excitement and nerves, "Pray to the gods for courage, boys! To glory!"

We became hounds, full of iron, and grit, but only in our minds. We had not seen real war, not yet. But we at least thought of ourselves as something different now, and one cannot change one's spirit until this transformation of the mind occurs — without deep conviction a man remains forever the same.

High upon the mountains, we needed to find the Cave of Souls, at the end of a rocky path through the hills that we had not yet taken. The second path. This would be the proof of our worth.

The tunnels beneath the peaks are so vast and so dark that even Myrmidon pathfinders have found themselves lost within the countless twists and turns. We had heard the rumors and the gossip about the creatures in the tunnels, but now we were ready to die in the pursuit of ourselves. We had reached a point in training where the consequences of failure seemed far worse than death.

Teris spoke first.

"This will take the absolute totality of your will. Your undivided suffering will end here. Your tent has served as a base for the strength of the unit to mend your wounds. You must face the trial to become a Myrmidon, as we all have."

Iesos reiterated the lesson of the lake. "A man is not a man until he comes to contend with the most destructive and deadly force he knows — the voice, the other, which lives in the Tartarus of each soul. Though all know this voice, few confront it."

"This tea…" growled Deimos, as he pointed to a cauldron boiling on the sand. It smelled like lavender and thyme and its smoke rose in twists. It was disturbing and yet comforting… "It will simulate your evils. For this reason, I cannot explain to you that which you will face, for I do not know what dark corners of the psyche you might visit. What will be clear to us is whether you possess the will to win against all foes. To become a Myrmidon, you must become a godlike warrior, in that you must be the most human you can be — the one who fights for more than what he sees before him. We will evaluate that determination has become a habit, and that when the seas of expiry come to wash through you at the height of the storm you stand firm. When the winds run, when the vicious waves roll high above your head, and there is nothing coming for you but the unyielding darkness, you merely laugh in the face of peril, and pull the tattered and ripped sails of your sinking ship higher, sailing towards the darkest part of the night."

We roared like lions. We clenched our ragged hands and felt the steel and the worn leather of our belts in our calloused palms. In all our notions of heavenly ascendence, of our transformation into killers, it was grounding to grasp the garments we wore. Closing our eyes, the whispers of the wind brushed against our cheeks, warm from the sea. It brought us from the abstract heights of ascendence back to the earth, where the work still lay ahead. The path was not yet conquered.

Our hands shook in passion and fear, but more than anything, we awaited the ultimate test. It could be that the rite of passage we craved brought us as close to death as possible. Men miss war because in those moments of unfiltered proximity to the heavens they felt alive.

Separated into groups of three, we made our way to the start of our path, in pursuit of Tartarus.

Grouped with Achilles and Pyrros, my fortunes of fate equalized among their attributes.

I wondered what might await us past the chambers, in the deep wells of our fears. We gulped the draught willingly and in succinct slugs.

I expected an immediate effect. Nothing took hold of me.

As we drank, Iesos spoke to us.

"You will find, on your path and in your life, that the demon preventing immediate action is not the enemy you see before you, but rather the one who burrows in your mind. In the abyss, do not make the mistake of believing you are alone, even if it is only the darkness staring back at you. Though the peaks of the mountains may seem close, you must first descend to the darkness below, in order to find the heights you seek, and you must face the things you would least prefer to face. Whatever creatures you may encounter, do not forget that they are manifestations of your personal fears, and for that reason you must not discount them as false. Some of you may only find the monster in yourself. Take the dirt path laid out here before you and find the cave you shall need to enter. Hades awaits you, young men."

With these words, we strode the path to destiny.

Upon that hill, the tea that seeped into my blood made me lucid, and light. Despite the severity of the moment, I could die in peace if the gods wished it, for I was in the company of my allies, in the grips of my syndicate of souls.

III

MIRRORS

As our trio walked the path, we said nothing to each other. Each boy was on guard. The wind brought the sour smell of pine through our midst. Familiarity calmed my nerves. Even if my mind shifted, the smell of the pine was something ingrained in me.

Pyrros almost immediately took off by himself. We hurried to stay by his side, for those were the rules set forth to us, but he did not care. "Pathetic," he spat back at us as we struggled to catch him. "The last thing I need is the likes of you two slowing me down."

The path itself was not arduous besides the burning in our legs. No creatures came before us there. We continued along with haste, but he did not have the patience to wait for us. Pyrros had little time for weakness, and so he had left us. Achilles and I spoke for the first time since his injury.

Achilles turned to me. "Hurry up."

"Be cautious, my friend," I noted.

"I do not fear death," he answered. His pupils widened, and his skin glistened with sweat despite the mild breeze.

"Then fear the gods," I rebutted.

"Who?" he replied, as if he did not understand the tongue in which I spoke.

"The gods."

He stopped. He did not look at me, but kept his gaze locked on the ground in front of him.

"My mother was one of them. Thetis was her name. She guided sailors across the vast ocean, until she fell in love with a ship captain, so she told me. The Myrmidons picked me up from an island called Syros." For a second, he had broken free from his torment.

"Thetis is the goddess of the sea, no?" Teris had taught us this. "Then you are half-god, and in you there are those qualities of the divine."

"Truthfully, I think not. I have heard the stories of my fate. I believe none of it. I was born poor. Gods wear armor of gold. I wore what was available to me in my poor life, and I have never felt godly. Since poverty, I've felt only the sting of the sword, and the cold grip of the world, and so, here I am with you."

He continued, "There is nothing divine in this path. There is nothing godly about losing, or misery. Olympus does not endorse me. I am doing nothing of merit. I am only trying not to die."

His eyes saddened. And in that moment, I realized that the burden of my life was lowly compared to his. If only I had asked earlier. If only I had stepped back from my own pain to take notice of a hurt greater than mine, which existed within him. This boy, broken, and carrying this fractured identity, had far worse to endure. I was fortunate in a way; I knew no parents nor siblings. I never knew those who birthed me. His soul was ripped from them. A broken child he was, the same as I, but he had endured much worse. I put my hand on his shoulder as he sighed.

The tea we had drunk was swirling in our minds; of this I was certain. Pyrros was far out of sight. He had no time for our philosophy. Achilles looked at me, and I him. We decided in that silence that that moment would be the time to stand, and not to falter, as every path has two directions, and a measurable end.

That made our lives simple. To climb or fall.

I turned to Achilles in his enveloping despair. I said what came naturally to me in the moment.

"We are all gods, those who do not quit, and who do not withdraw in the face of their fears and doubts. Those who do not doubt their history but embrace it. We who are fragile. There is nothing heroic about natural valor when one only acts valorous. It is an unassuming act for the naturally heroic man to act with courage. But we know how arduous the path can be. And so, a hero who has never broken will not survive when the inevitable break occurs. Only men who know fracture finish the fight, and only the men who know true despair can act heroic. In this way, you are the most heroic of us, for what you've lost and for how you are still standing."

That was the most important moment, the lowest one. It was at that time that we would either hold ourselves against all the evil in the world, or give in to our base instincts, and act as children do. Stay boys or become men in the responsibility we would have to undertake.

In our ascending violence, in our unaltered brutality, we retained responsibility over everything in our lives, so that we did not become monsters. I look back now at those idyllic days, the hard ones. The sun would still rise and glow orange through the windows of the morning. It told us that the day still held purpose for us. We learned idealism through pain, and we learned that true times of peace are only earned through suffering. We learned to understand chaos so that we might deal with it more calmly when we found ourselves in the inferno.

He nodded silently in the breeze. We lowered our heads and strained our boots forward to slice the beaten dirt that lined the path. Ahead we heard the faintest whisper of Pyrros' solo progress. And, despite our advance into the unknown, we could still hear the crash of the familiar ocean waves against the sandy shore, now far, far below us.

We knew then we neared the cave, far along the mountain path upon which we treaded. Under the evening sun we moved our feet towards fate. As the liquid I consumed dispersed in my veins and became part of my blood, the trees began to sway in my vision. I knew this was not yet the worst of the things to come.

The trees were the ancient things of the world. They had watched all of the glory and the tragedy, and they had seen us corrode before. They stood in the place they always had. Now, they appeared to move, to turn towards me, to judge my momentary presence on a world they had inhabited for centuries. I felt small, but the kind of small that makes up a part of the larger things. I saw the leaves breathe and radiate in the sunshine. A synchronous breath between us matched the rise and fall of my own lungs. All the while, the dust of the trail remained hanging in the air.

As the mix I had consumed took hold, I saw lush trees, healthy and green, turn quickly to ash. Absent of fire or storm but burnt from their roots, I watched as the wind blew away the remains of the oak. The wind carried them, never to know their homes again but to make their place somewhere else in the world.

The longer I walked the more abhorrent the visions became. Achilles' eyes darted unnaturally, and I assumed his mind was soaring as well. Soon, the heat from the sun disappeared, and the black forest attacked the trees that still had their green life. The corrupted trees turned on their fellow saplings. Shrubs ripped and thrashed the life from their uncorrupted comrades, and their pine needles went flying into the air. Now, murdered by their compatriots, the smell of detached pine lingered heavy upon the breeze.

Achilles looked at me, and I him, but we dared not speak of our visions. We walked together, on guard and prepared for a shadowy enemy. We were afraid, wary of the conjurings of our mind and the malevolence that lurked beneath our hearts. We had heard the warning clear — all men have darkness within them.

The deterioration of my mind was vicious. The trees' black branches fell to the ground before us and turned to serpents. Hissing, fangs bared, they lunged at our ankles. We broke into a run. The snakes chased us relentlessly. As in a horrid dream my legs were heavy, my reactions blunted, and my voice, in its desperate attempt to scream and yell choked and gagged. I wondered if my inability came from fear, or from a deep desire or force that was coaxing me into bravery.

My bravery was not the complete absence of fear, as I had to act in the face of such horror, even if the courageous act was to run. As I turned my head to verify my pursuers, I saw that it was not one nor two poisonous creatures, but hundreds.

Rounding the final turn, I saw the crack in the earth that marked our destination. All at once, the hissing, which had dissolved into the subtle sounds of the wind and the sea, stopped, and I was alone.

Achilles was gone.

Deimos appeared like a ghost and stepped down from a rock on the hillside. He said no words to me. Instead, he handed me a torch, already lit with a brilliant flame. He pointed towards the pit. It was unnerving to see a man of anger so quiet.

The pit. There lay my entry to the underworld. It lurked beneath the island all this time.

In all my helpless nightmares I could not have pictured a fouler place.

Smoke rose from the desolate fracture in the earth. The dark called to me, murmuring in a foreign tongue, and it was in that moment I knew that I must go. Harnessing the courage to descend into obscurity, I stepped forward. Though terrified and anxious of what might await me, this destiny, like the tides of the Aegean, dragged me below the hellish surface.

My torch lit the cramped hall before me. The tunnel was carved from ancient earth. Water dripped from the rotting wood which held the roof, and the brass from the bolts had rusted away and sent cascading strips of auburn down the wall to where the ankle-deep water sat stagnant, disturbed only by the footsteps of the hopeful boys who had trod there before, and now by me.

The stench was overwhelming. It was that of rotting meat left out too long in camp, ripped apart by wolves and half-eaten by maggots. The corridor was long and narrow, and though the water dripped from the roof, the oily torch in my hand stayed lit. Soon my clothes and my armor became wet from the steady trickle of the falling water, and my equipment felt far heavier upon my back.

As I moved along the passageway, I stopped. Ahead, in the darkened tunnel, five or six feet in front of me, something disturbed the stillness of the water. The water continued to ripple as the expanding figure of a creature slithered its way below the icy surface. Of all the monsters my potion could bring, I knew not what it might be, but what it had to be: the thing I feared the most, the serpent.

I turned around to check my exit and nothing greeted me but a solid wall of dirt, wet to the touch and immovable as a mountain. My way was forward, then. I tried to clear my mind of the creatures slithering in the dark. Drawing my sword provided me comfort. Its familiar weight felt like a friend. The torch's light glinted off the blade and shimmered in the reflection of the water, lighting the way.

Grip tightening on the leather of the handle, I pushed on, careful and slow. I kept my vision on the darkness, ready for anything that might strike.

I arrived at a crossroads of tunnels, a meeting place of the canals, and this provided me with a choice of the three entryways.

Each tunnel bore an emblem above its entrance, but that would be the only sign I would receive.

The first resembled a beautiful woman, sat upon a rock in the sea.

The second appeared to me as a labyrinth, with a bull's head resting upon its middle.

On the third stood a snakelike creature, with many twisted terrorizing heads and fangs like knives. This tore my soul to pieces and caused my hands to shake. It was a Hydra, spoken of by Teris. In an instant I knew. And down the dark corridor I walked, wary of the impending encounter of the beast but certain of my feet and the steel that I held.

As in a dream, the world surrounded me with truth. And yet, despite my best efforts to recognize that the structure that encircled me was safe, I took my actions as if the real-life consequences were still a threat. That corridor was very much like my life, where my dreams appeared sometimes more believable and harsher than my reality. This battle with the monster would mean that the rest of my life would be simple. If I could muster the courage the face the unknown, then the battle would only be a matter of moving forwards or backwards.

But I came to find that men are far worse than monsters.

A single torch lit the end of the long passageway. The hallway opened up into a rock-laden pit. There was no ceiling, only the open sky of the night. As I approached, the fire of my torch raged in a howling wind, which doused the flame. Fragments of light reflected from the stone, engulfed in the moonlight.

There were no alternative exits. The only reprieve from the rigid stone was a pool, full of crystal-blue water, which sat in the middle of the enormous stone cage. The water was as still as the rock surrounding it. I edged closer to the water, for I had no other route, nor destination.

Stacked twenty stones high and bonded with hard, old marble, the pit showed its age. Where the marble had eroded and cracked there were stains. Dried blood. It had found its way into the tiny fissures of the compacted floor. Many battles had taken place here.

On the decisive step at the water's edge, the surface swelled and gurgled. The foam rose. I took two steps back, but the water exploded with a rage so devastating that the rocks seemed to shake against its presence. I did not flee, nor shake, nor even shudder in the midst of the chaos, because I knew already what lay beneath the calm water. I was soaked from the passageway before. Turning my head away from the chaos, the water cascaded down the top of my helmet and pelted the bronze shoulders of my armor. I kept my eyes shut tight, awaiting the end of the rupture.

I tasted the salt, though I was far from the shores. Opening my eyes, I saw the glare of yellow eyes strike towards me, and, grasping my sword and shield, time ceased. Suspended in the longest moment I have ever endured as a man, the Hydra, its fangs bearing down on me and its eyes, angry like mine had been as a child, wanted death. The three heads of the serpent swirled and howled in the moonlight. It stood as a giant before me. Its heads writhed, a muscular deep blue, and black shields lined its scales. They rippled against the light of the moon. I remember the droplets of water hanging in the air. I remember, as I would for the rest of my life as a warrior, the feeling of the heft of my sword and the calm sensation that it sent throughout my body.

Something pierced the smooth skin of my arm, and my body went rigid, paralyzed by the excrutiating pain. From my right arm the life poured from me. Blood spurted like a crimson waterfall. My vision ebbed. Before the overwhelming darkness, and before all the light of the world left, I saw a glint of gold hair, the glare of yellow eyes, and I saw the blood, my blood, spray against the grey plaster which held the walls.

I resigned myself to death once more. I lost control. The pit echoed with the sound of my armor and body as they smashed the cold stone. "Bring me to Elysium. Carry me across to the distant coastline. I shall wait for my brothers there," I pleaded to the air.

I awoke still in the damp cave. Though I was alive, my arm seared with pain as if in a crushing vice. When I looked down, I saw the distinctive punctures from the fangs of a great snake. The web of veins running through my arm had turned purple and red. They pumped venom through my limbs and towards my heart. The river of blood coming from my wounds separated in the running water of the pool. The snake laid motionless, half in and half out of its lair. Dead.

And with my sword stuck deep into its midsection, only the glint of the handle showed, but the sword was mine all the same.

In all my acute observation, I did not notice that it was Achilles tending the wounds in my arm. Pyrros was not in the pit with us.

"What happened?" I stuttered.

"You saved me," he replied.

"I saved you?"

"Yes. The moment the snake was about to strike, you dove into the pool and stuck your sword in its heart, but it reeled and one of its heads ripped your arm apart. I pulled you out of the water, but I was certain you were dead. Your body was limp… you were with the gods."

"I may die."

"I would be dead if you hadn't acted. I cowered at the beast."

But I could die here now, and that would be fine; it was better than on the mountain. Even in its falsehood, what I had done had the merit of warriorship. And it had been for a brother of mine, so whatever challenge the gods might present in the afterlife, I was certain that I could judge myself as up to the task — as a man of character.

The slow closing of my eyes, like the going down of the evening sun, comforted my fading soul. Darkness came once more, but before it could take me, lightning broke the sky and the black canvas of stars above me cracked, like a warming ice in spring.

In a flash of heavenly rage, a man appeared before us, battle ready. His gold armor clung to his muscular figure. The rearing horse depicted on his breastplate shone in the moonlight. On his hip was a sheathed sword. He drew his ancient weapon, which echoed into the empty pit. But unlike the rest of his armor, which was crisp and clean, the sword itself showed heavy signs of battle.

In that moment we knew who had come to address us — Ares — god of War, and so, god of us.

In an instant, the god we loved confirmed our fate. His voice commanded attention and devastated the stillness of the dome.

"It is true," he spoke to us, "death finds you."

And we bowed our heads and smiled at the hallowed ground.

"But not the death you know. You have buried that which you once were, the boys you used to be, the naïve souls of those who do not know just how violent the world can be. You, in your endurance, have broken your bonds of mediocrity and answered the call, and in doing so, you have proven your position. Though no god should meddle in the world of men, your wounds heal by my hand, and your ranks solidify by my authority."

He turned to Achilles and said, "A warrior."

And then to me to continue, "And an officer of the Myrmidons; for only officers bear the mark, the scar, that demonstrates the ultimate sacrifice."

Now that I looked down at the once devastating injury, I saw that the skin had closed and calloused. The serpent slithered as my healed skin moved. Etched in black, this symbol wrote a new destiny upon my arm. It was a gift from Ares, and one I treasured above all things. Though I was proud, I questioned my ability, as all men do.

"What grants me such a privilege?"

He looked at me.

"There is nothing we value more than sacrifice, besides courage, and sacrifice is a mere subsidiary of courage. Do not mistake this for honor; honor is something we as warriors all share and which we revel in. This position is one of heartache and pain and can be taken away from you as quickly as it given out. Our officers serve the men. They seek no additional comforts nor merits. If they do seek such things, we strip them immediately of their position. We promote them to bear the shield at the front of the line, so that they may regain their humility in their proximity with death.

"Only when a warrior cares about his comrades above himself can he assume this role. As he is not yet a father of children, this sacrifice is the ultimate test of leadership, for he must love his men like the sons he does not have.

"An officer expires for his men first, and himself last. He almost never finds peace for himself. It is a cruel and unjust life for the individual soul but valiant and crucial to the team. Such is the life of leaders."

I could ask him no further questions, for the god was gone as rapidly as he had appeared.

IV

NAIVETY

We exited the pit by climbing the smooth rocks, as we had on the wall with Teris. As we pulled our bodies over the ledge, roars of triumph erupted from behind us. Pyrros and the other boys stood in clean, tight ranks, fifteen feet away. Their black armor gleamed menacingly under the night's sky.

The mentors approached Achilles and I, one at a time. In their hands, they held black shields, greaves, breastplates, and swords which harnessed the night. They placed the armor in the arms of Achilles, who took his place in the line. Deimos approached with mine, his usual look of anger replaced by something only slightly softer.

"Stelios," he said to me.

Addressed as "boy" by the mentors for years, and not even allowed the dignity of an identity on the farm, the sound of my name shot adrenaline through my veins. I realized in that moment that it was the first time I was proud of it. Quite a lesson for a man to learn.

"Myrmidons." Teris addressed us as such for the first time. It rang like lightning in our ears. "Time to join your brothers in arms."

We left the next morning. Our mentors left with us. A new team of Myrmidons would arrive to train the new recruits. The mentors of training cycles stayed with the team, so that the strong bond forged in the crucible between instructor and student could then translate to the battlefield. It was a tactic developed over years of trial and error.

Again, it was a vessel that carted us to the other side of our lives. It cut through the ocean like a sword through flesh. The spray from the breaking waves dried our skin and left white crystals upon our arms. The salt took its place upon the clean black armor we wore. Not all of the boys made it through the trials, but their possessions remained. We stood in line, and without saying a word, we dropped the trinkets they had once cherished into the depths.

As the shoreline faded from view, I wondered if I would ever return. The beaches and forests of that place were soaked in the sweat and blood of young aspiring soldiers. Our mentors had become an eternal piece of forging lost youth into the elite ranks, and I wished for the same reward.

As we sailed from our island to the main camp, visions of a beautiful future came to me upon the wisps of the ocean spray. The sea danced and brought to me a prophecy. Upon the mist I saw battles. Lucid as a memory, but tactile, like the ridges of a leather belt, they manifested before my eyes. Glorious victories sat layered between the crests and troughs of the sea.

But they vanished as the frigid air of the sea took over.

Along the voyage Deimos spoke to me, his gruff voice startling me as I looked out over the expanse. "Sir… This is your first lesson after all the lessons. Our lives as Myrmidons are almost always the ability to deal with constant suffering." His words were clean.

"What comes beyond that?"

"Peace, I think. Though I have not found it for myself yet," he pondered. "But bear these discomforts for as long as you can, so others with gentler hearts need not to."

Though we sailed the blue ocean the same as we had as boys, we held ourselves differently now. Each man's shining black armor glinted in the wake of the rudder, leaving the ocean and their histories behind. I noticed that some of them bore similar marks to myself, though with slight differences. One man, Kleitos, had the bite of a great predator imprinted upon his thigh. Another, Nikephoros, bore the webbed mark of the spider. Each man, with each manifestation of the things that frightened them the most, had faced their fears with courage.

I wondered if they had met Ares — they must have, their wounds had healed like mine. But I wondered if they felt the crushing weight of responsibility as I now did. In our culture we did not speak of personal moments; we did not need to shout them to the world. We took them for ourselves, as opportunities in which to change.

Alexius leaned close and whispered to me on the sail, "You are, beyond a doubt, the ugliest officer I have ever seen."

"You have seen no others," I whispered.

"Yes. The bar has been set that low, my friend," he laughed back.

Iesos prayed for us as we rowed. He was a calming man, who could soothe a wild boar into slumber, but who, when called forth, could bring the strength of hell with him. That is why I respected the man, why I held him in such high regard. His voice carried across the Aegean and his belief never faltered.

"Men, the movement of the sea harnessed by the great trident brings forth all the things a man wonders about himself, but it is best at bringing forth his doubts. To change that which we know about ourselves we must first doubt how much responsibility we think we can shoulder. If a man does not reflect on this fact or on his life, he will not see that he has already changed in the most important fashion — he has built himself, stone by stone. A man must understand that while he is already winning the war against himself by building the wall, the wall must never finish."

We saw that our greatest power came not in our swordcraft or strength; it came through our ability to find positivity in adversity. It was the ability to deal with the inexplicable wavering way of life — its instability became our strength. In our new lives, the cold, the heat, the lack, the excess, and all the hostility we knew merely became a single wavelength by which we all functioned. Deal with all things the same, and do not protest nor complain. Instead of a raft floating lifelessly, destined to sway and journey with the changing desires of the sea, we had crafted oak oars. We could row the day and the night atop the powerful sea.

Our hands were rough now. Familiar with the splinters, the blisters and callouses hardened.

We would never quit, which is an easy thing to say but a damned hard thing to do. It was a useful skill for a soldier to learn and to master. It allowed us to do our jobs and to do them well. But tuning out the world in such a way also meant we never fully accepted the things we did, and this haunted some of the hardest men.

The sun had set. The men continued to row, slicing the oars in rhythm. The carved and polished brown paddles disappeared in motion below the surface. We took our turns rowing, officer and soldier alike, as equals. I had heard the stories of the Athenians and how their leaders slept in woven tents constructed by the men on the field of battle. I had listened carefully when Iesos explained that their hierarchy afforded these titles to the aristocratic men, whose fathers held high seats in government.

"Beware the anger that sparks in the hearts of front-liners when an officer sleeps longer upon his straw bed than he does in his bed of dirt, or when he eats fine salted pork rather than dried olives like his lower-ranking counterparts.

"We do not operate in this manner," he explained. "Our leaders cultivate respect. Even mighty trees rot if their roots begin to wrap around poisoned moss."

Evening had fallen on the ship. The men shifted in their seats as we approached the mainland. In the distance stood the twinkling lights of a peaceful town. Houses stood atop the hills, watching over us. It was a happiness I had never known at that age.

But it was not our job to think about happiness. Our eyes shifted to the army camp, which radiated something far different.

Our profession was war.

As we unloaded the linen packs that housed our gear, Iesos directed us to the main tent. The regiment we were to become a part of feasted together. Red wine crafted from Thessalian grapes flowed.

Each vine of Greece produces its own unique drink, and each batch affects the men of our country in distinct ways. One might think our vines are filled with the blood of fallen enemies, so that when we down the bowls of nectar, our fortitude strengthens, and our lust for death only grows more vengeful. Nothing could be further from the truth.

We entered the lion's den of then Myrmidons, where our growing confidence shattered once more. We again became mice, running helplessly around the paws of lions who toyed with us.

Where we expected seasoned experts of death, we also found brothers encapsulated in deep conversation. Where we expected seriousness, we found weathered warriors engulfed in laughter. One man had fallen from his bench and was so overtaken with humor that his body writhed in the dirt. This only spurred his brothers on.

We were out of place among the men who had spent their lives together, though we wore the same uniforms. And as we entered the tent with Iesos, the raucous stopped. The earth ceased to spin. The mass of men stood and eyed us. The silence was uncomfortable to the utmost degree.

But again, the men burst into laughter, and I admit I let a small smirk escape my face as a slight bit of relief washed over my body. The men came to greet us, and another, far more experienced officer than myself grabbed me by the shoulder and brought me to his table. He was tall, but wiry, with muscular legs that screamed their endurance to me — I would never once in my life beat him up the mountain.

He was the man who had delivered bedding to our camp, the one I had seen long ago.

"Kalliaros," he stated, extending his hand. He sat me down at the table with the other men. A grizzled soldier immediately began to ridicule me. "Hold your breastplate still, son, I need to shave my beard."

I smiled.

"You look like you think too much." He offered me his wine.

"Someone has to," I said.

Immediately I regretted this rebuttal. But this soldier, having been through the exact same ritual in his youth, laughed and applauded my pluck.

"Welcome." He laughed again and offered up his cup to a toast. "May we die quickly and soon," he said.

The other men raised theirs and replied in unison, "And together."

"And together," I added.

Alexius, whose humor was his greatest asset, and whose mind was light and carefree, integrated quickly with his table. He sat three rows from mine. Soon, my friend had the grown men spitting their food onto the table as they howled in laughter.

The wine continued to pour as night flooded the tent. Men had begun to slowly leave, in small groups, but I did not want to be rude. I did not even want to stand up, having made my comfortable home hidden at the table. When the last of our table left, it was just Kalliaros and I. As we swished the final drops of wine in our goblets and downed the red liquid, he became serious with me. His eyes met mine, and I could see the brown cracks and shades that led from his irises into the whites of his gaze.

"You did well tonight," he began, "but this is not a reflection of our lives. Do not speak of the trials; we have all been through them. They do not represent the truth of our lives."

I stayed silent, listening to the man.

"I've heard about the potential in you, Stelios."

I started to nod but his face turned stern.

"You have proven nothing to me yet."

He patted me on the back and left the tent, and there, among the mess of food, spilled wine, and cups, I sat alone.

He popped his head back into the tent and startled me.

"And clean this shit up," he added.

I laughed.

Each plateau reached was another opportunity to start at the lowest of the pack; being a soldier is a brutal life. The Myrmidons were hard men, forged in combat and brotherhood, whose characters and will rivaled the rigor of the steel they held. These warriors took an extreme amount of delight in hammering the metal of newcomers, though most of it was in jest. On the few occasions when true malice came forth, or when a prodding began to stray too far from its intended purpose, the others quickly reprimanded the guilty party.

Each trial required purpose.

As I laid my head down to sleep that night, my world spun. The fields of my youth attempted to grapple with the alcohol in the wine. I wanted to close my eyes, and rest, if only to silence my mind for a moment. I lay awake. My chest ached with pressure. It was the knowledge that, of all the men that night, I had earned such lighthearted evenings the least.

Deimos informed me the next day of the conflict in Rhodes.

In Rhodes, a revolt had risen up from the depths of the society. The revolution, led by Krakos, slaughtered the old guard and took the city by force. The island state was of tactical and strategic importance — it provided a forward base for operations into Persia. Standing watch at the harbor of the island state sat the Colossus, a statue of Helios, god of the Sun. In addition, the Colossus itself was a culturally significant piece of history.

When Krakos took control, he dispersed the city-dwellers to farm the interior. And when famine took the land, it was no surprise to the people of Greece; forced farming predicated on the ability of city-dwellers, and not on the ancient teachings of the few families who actually knew how to farm, was ill-advised and dangerous. Murdered were the successful farming families, whose tiny piece of happiness deemed them more privileged than the rest. Krakos slaughtered them like cattle, to purge the society of excess and wealth. And so, everyone else starved and died as equally as they had as a result. But Krakos insisted Rhodes subsist on pure economical gain.

Instead of excess, less food meant that more died, and those who remained hoarded what they could, and the more that hoarded the more he executed for their treason. So more died again. The island itself had of late rid its doctrine of any imperial allegiance in a communique to the directors of Greece. Threatening extreme violence for any army that dared to venture beyond the Colossus of Helios, Krakos made the island his own piece of hell. The land descended into chaos. Plumes of smoke sometimes traveled across the ocean, reaching the shores of Athens. And when the Greeks had to smell the burning bodies, it inconvenienced their day. Only then did they send us.

Only then did they care.

The Myrmidons, along with a Greek battalion of mercenaries, reported to clean up the mess. We drilled our tactics, our flanking movements, and all of our other grand killing innovations.

"I am sure, Zeus, that other men who have visited this temple have outlined these methods of war, but I feel that you have not summoned me here to hear such things…"

"Men have arrived here hoping to impress the gods with their military procedures. These abilities make no impressions on our eternal lives. We have seen too many years pass, too many inventions of war. What remains constant is the bloodlust men hold in their hearts for each other," Zeus noted.

"And glory is limited by the time we are granted on earth. Yet we hunted for such things like beasts." To his left, Stelios noticed a crack in one of the pillars. As he turned slightly to look, an old wound flared in his side.

Though my first night led me to believe different, I soon saw the truth of the matter: age and experience divided our ranks. Whatever notions we had of glory soon clashed with the attitude of the men who had experienced a lifetime of violence.

I first saw this in preparation for the war in Rhodes. Young warriors sparred with intensity and grit as they trained for the coming conflict. In their eyes stood the reckoning of the foe; in their hands, the sweat poured as they gripped their weapons. Enthusiasm drove them. A lust to prove themselves. The youth, myself included, spoke of the valiant fight, the noble battle, where we would earn our places.

The older warriors shook their heads at us. They looked, but they needn't scold. We would come to learn in time.

A grizzled man did approach me after Leandros got too boisterous and loud. Unconcerned with my rank, he said, "Get these boys in line, *sir*, they speak of matters they know nothing of."

I took his advice.

I felt that we did something noble for the people. I expected the same acceptance from the citizens outside of war. But I was mistaken. In truth, I came to learn that dissent and anger in soldiers stems from having no rightful place to call home.

We are not to blame. It was not our fault. We were soldiers when they needed us…

They loved us when war came, but when the memory of war faded, they never quite trusted us. The old men always respected us. The young adults looked at us and embraced us, but we were stray dogs to them. I don't blame them. When we went away, they settled into their routines with their families, and they laughed with joy. The town went about its business as usual. Children studied. Parents worked. And after work and school, the fathers kissed their sons and hugged their daughters and told them of their day. That was the type of man they knew.

And we were somewhere far away, covered in blood.

When we came home, we couldn't explain to those who lived so peacefully just how brutal war was, because it defeated the purpose of soldiers. Our profession was to bear that which sickens the soul, and which cannot be described. We couldn't explain it to them, because, truly, they didn't want to know.

But because we knew our lives were fleeting, we drank like the sun would not rise again. Screaming, yelling, and howling with laughter at the *kapeleia*, the citizens looked at us with worry. All we were trying to do was drown the memories of our friends. We couldn't act like everyone else. We tried.

And when we walked past their daughters and sons, they placed their hands on the shoulders of the beautiful children and moved them to the other side of the road. We grinned at them; our smiles were genuine. They smiled back at us politely and briefly, but they didn't keep eye contact long. They assumed that all we loved was pain, and that we only knew how to be brash and intense — we never even considered these things about ourselves because we were too busy trying to forget everything else.

They thought we were horrific men who did horrific things, and they were right. But we never wished to do these things. We never asked for such violent lives.

We went far from home. Our eyes glazed over as we witnessed things young men should not. The longing for our beds burned with a passion that ignited the embers in our chests. The pain of being gone twisted our bones. It was all we could do in each moment not to break down and weep, so we thought as little as possible. We only thought about the sound of the *salpinx*, which told us to stop.

And then, when we finally got home, they looked at us and smiled politely again. But later, in the comfort of their homes, when they thought we could not hear them, they said to each other, "Why are soldiers such beasts? Can they not act more civilized?"

As if it were some curtain we could draw over our agony.

The angriest men had seen the most of the world. Nestled deep in the scars of their armor was an intense nihilism. Older warriors moved through their day far differently than we did. A more solemn attitude overtook them. Something sinister lurked below. Their bodies showed the corruption and weathering of their age.

We held no beautiful illusions of the world either — we had been born into slavery and captured by its monotony. These men knew this, and they did not care. They had seen a lifetime of war. At one point they had been hopeful and charismatic like us, but at another, they had broken and become pessimistic about the state of the world they found themselves in. They changed. They stopped reflecting on where they came from. This is dangerous in powerful men and especially in soldiers, because in times where the threat of death becomes imminent, they hold reservations deep in their mind about what exactly they are dying for. In turn these men purposefully sour relationships, push away those who love them, and interact as if they knew the world was corrupt all along, and everyone was blind not to see it.

It was not because of evil. It was because men rarely do that which they most need to do in life — find out exactly who they are in each moment. Earning the black armor was only the beginning of the journey, but it did not fortify a man into morality or heroism; it gave him a solid foundation from which to build himself.

But what warriors need most in the world is someone to explain to them what exactly peace is. It might've saved us all. We never started the wars, but we always suffered because of them.

And paradoxically it is easy to be confident and filled with purpose while fighting — it is addictive. It is far more difficult to take a hard look at oneself after the fact. To admit that we made incorrect decisions was far more arduous. Our misguided motivations, the ones we thought we believed, were a challenging thing to own.

There was purpose in upholding the codes we created, but what challenged us was being able to align these warrior codes with the ambitions of political power and exploitation. As soldiers of the state we were always expected to uphold things we did not believe in. But in combat, as in all things, the situations are complex, and cluttered. Where we found purpose in reducing misery, we also found exploitation and greed. A genocide might be stopped, but only if the land held some resource useful to the state; these things existed together like a bee and a flower. In the end, there was always some reason to go and fight which tugged upon the code of ethics we had sewn into our very fiber, but it always also aligned with the ambitions of rulers. We remained purposefully blind to some of the more menacing motivations.

We prepared to leave for Rhodes in a fortnight's time, and until then we had liberty to live in the nearby town that sat beside the Pineios River. The stream flowed along the eastern shores of the town. It provided a refuge for warriors and children alike to swim and to drink from.

"What if the men never come back?" I asked Kalliaros. "It seems foolish to give such freedoms to such highly trained and drilled soldiers."

We sat in front of an anthill. The tiny insects carried leaves into the mound of dirt and disappeared into the countless tunnels they'd made. Below the surface was a complex world we could not see, though it seemed simpler than ours.

"This strategy of leniency is far from foolish," he replied. "Though some believe that soldiers who partake in the overconsumption of alcohol and pleasure are certain to never return, this is untrue to its core. To constantly drive men to strengthen, like swords forged in fire, is only useful to the point of its greatest strength. Like steel used for the blade, men have a breaking point. In the steel it is the point where the smith smashes the metal once too many times. The forger notices this because the sparks that fly from the burning steel begin to change. Without the cold barrel and a reprieve from constant and relentless crushing and altering, the sword loses its sharpness and density. And though some men do not return, the ones who do fight harder as they needed a reprieve from war."

"And we do not hunt the deserters down? We do not condemn them for leaving their brothers stranded on the field of battle?" I asked.

"We have no need of the ones who fail to return, and so we make no effort to locate them. A Myrmidon soldier has no contract that requires that he stay — only a moral contract that if he returns, he does so ready for battle. If he does not, it is because he has a found a love worthy of leaving his brothers for, or because he has seen too much of war."

I looked at him, confused.

He replied to my expression, "There is such a thing, my friend, even for us.

"And if he does leave, it is his reward, the thing he fought for in the first place. This is why we let the men leave in times of peace, so they may gain insight into the things for which they sacrifice themselves. Otherwise, life is all war and preparation for war. And the reasons for combat disappear with the sunset — mere dust upon the trail of life. In contrast we find peace, but the kind of warrior peace found after time spent in the fire, and because we give everything for each other, we savor their personal victories, and our brothers' peace becomes ours to hold as well.

"So, when the war drums finally do sound, we fight with even more fervent hatred for our enemies and even more love for our friends."

But his eyes did not leave the dying sunset.

I sometimes spent the evening with Alexius, but that included more of me listening and him speaking. My mind would shift with the currents, swirling with the ebbs and flows of the icy water as he joked.

I spent my days dining and drinking on the banks of the swift-flowing river. I did not seek the comforts of women or friends. I saw Achilles many times. I tried to reach out to him. "Achilles, my friend. How does the morning treat you?"

"The same, Stelios." He refused to reveal any emotion. Pyrros had taken something from him.

It was like grasping at the sunrays breaking through a woodland cloaked in dusk.

Families swam during the long days. I cheered and clapped when the children learned to tread water. Life was almost always the ability to rejoice in small victories. Their expressions gave me something that training for war had always lacked. It settled the storm inside my stomach.

Achilles was there, but he was not the same boy I once knew. He retreated back into his new coldness.

His personal loss, the one of his mother, must have been hiding down below, waiting. I had little to lose during my youth, and so, my transformation was one of requirement, and not of force.

When I saw him pass throughout the town, we would nod and smile at one another. He spent his time with Chrysanthe, the widow of a Myrmidon named Aegeus, whose son was no older than six. The boy was charming, and polite, and he adored Achilles. Achilles thought the world of him. I thought that in some way he might be trying to save this child's life from his own fate, but it was much more than that.

One morning, I saw them out walking, and while Chrysanthe and Achilles walked along the path, the boy jumped from stone to stone, as children do. Upon the final piece of rock wall, the boy missed his mark and stumbled. He fell from the wall. I saw the face of Achilles. The man I called my brother rushed to the child's side, as he would do for a dying comrade in war. He picked up the youth, and angrily kicked the rock wall. It shattered with such devastating rage that pieces of rock sprayed against the side of the home to whom it belonged.

His reaction took me aback. The wall was small and held no danger to the boy. Children jumped upon it every day that I had been in the village; it was what children did. But his overreaction granted me a window into the pain of his youth, and it demonstrated to me how the man I knew loved his family. He wanted to protect them from all the things in the world from which he hadn't been. But life will never grant a man this ideal. Holding on to something with such an obsessive tightness is destructive when the inevitable moment approaches and one's grip begins to break.

Achilles loved them. As he taught the young boy to swim in the river, his golden hair gleamed in the warm Greek sunshine. There was an unmistakable connection between them. Destiny united them, in that moment together. All the while, Chrysanthe smiled and laughed, and the laugh lines in her face ached with the passing of time since she had laughed last. She was elegant, but tough as a front-ranker. Her sharp features reminded us of our weapons, and her dark brown eyes appraised us, unyielding. Her spirit knew war, and her heart, the loss of a soldier and a husband. But she understood, more than most men, the sacrifices life often demands.

I started to hope that Achilles would find that thing that Kalliaros spoke to me of, that he would never come back to the battalion. But, in the way that life is so cruel, I was wrong.

Achilles had met her on our third day in the small village, before we had all left each other to find solitude in our attempts to reconcile the upcoming combat in our minds. His golden hair, now long and braided, sat to the side of his blue eyes. The lines on his cheeks grew more prominent, and I was glad to see that, though the man was a god, he still aged like us. He was impossible to miss, however, and I always saw him with her, and with love in his eyes. I was happy for him, though I knew that war was in his blood.

Myrmidons have no obligation to fight. I've mentioned this, but Achilles, driven by his upbringing and his origin, knew that war and everything it brought forth would keep him happy enough to return to Chrysanthe. He also knew that staying in peace would only make him angry enough to leave forever.

Those days spent on the riverside remained some of my best days. But the mediocrity of the daily routine ate away at me like running water against stone. I had no reason to be angry, for I lived a charmed life of fresh food and red wine in the sunshine, and yet, my blood boiled beneath the surface. Beautiful things surrounded me — I wanted to destroy them. I could not envision a future where I would crave peace. I resisted the urge to scream and yell. Without war, I should've been content. When the river was quiet and cold, without the laughter of the children or the mumbled conversation of those in love, I felt troubled. Each night, the seams which I had fixed during the day became undone again. It was unexplainable. I was young.

Only exercise seemed to calm my feelings, but soon even that was not enough. I began my day with early runs through the trails that snaked the mountainside. I found unity in the impact of my feet on the dirt and the beating of my heart in my chest. And when I reached the top of the trail, I would sit for a few moments and watch the treetops in the breeze.

But because not every day is simple, sometimes my mind would wander and turn to darkness. In my life, I have seen that even the greatest warriors and the most powerful men have, on some days, immense self-doubt. This is an inevitable part of our existence, and though all men have it, only some work through it. But the world renews. If a man can work hard and still make it to his bed that evening, he will wake up with a better perspective and attitude, while still accomplishing the things he needed to during his day of internal darkness. It does not last forever, but it requires grit and determination to push through such pain.

There was one peaceful morning following my run, when the clouds billowed and adopted the gentle white of the breaking sea. For a moment I thought I grasped a bit of peace, but the world turned cold. The glinting sunshine that broke the surface of the powerful river vanished and turned black. The clear water turned to sludge. The pieces of mud churned by the feet of children slid below its depths and poisoned the once beautiful river. Inside, my heart screamed. The falling pink blossoms from the tress turned to blowing snow, and the children disappeared below the ripples. The houses became desolate, deserted, and in a flash, they turned from homes to fiery infernos that melted the surrounding snow. I was alone on my tiny piece of earth, still sitting on the trail. Achilles appeared across the river, staring blankly at me, before the fire engulfed him. I screamed a plea. At first it seemed silent, but in an instant, I realized I was manic, and the echoes of my cries rang throughout the valley.

I snapped back to reality. The children stopped swimming. They stared at me in horror, and I left the riverside in the hopes I would not frighten anyone else.

Zeus spoke, *"Hades calls to you, Myrmidon. He is cunning, and ruthless, my brother of the deep. Here he presents you a vision of chaos — the chaos that sends its sirens to you in times of peace. The sovereign of the underworld often seeks men like you. He knows intimately the men who use swords as their authority. He knows they seek to be rulers of madness, but he forgets that some men would rather die honorably than be king of nothing."*

The Myrmidon glanced over his shoulder, expecting the demon to be, as it had always been, waiting in the dark for him. The hall was empty save for the breeze. "It is a dangerous thing, to tempt such men. It is cathartic, at first, to tear the world apart."

This image exited as quickly as it had appeared, for it was only in my mind. But after my trials I knew how powerful the mind was, and how our realities are not quite what they might appear. I realized that my little refuge, my piece of paradise, was an alternate to what was possible. It was our decisions that dictated such things. I knew then that I could not control everything in my world, but I could control how I approached the things I could not influence. Realizing that as much as we build our sanctuaries, we construct our anguish as well, I walked the path home. Our little pieces of hell are far closer than they appear, given the wrong choices by men, while our pieces of heaven are in reach, though we rarely extend our hands to hold them.

When I got home, I pulled out the fabric of my old sail from long ago, and my breathing slowed.

I sought out Alexius for some reprieve. I found him drinking wine with the elderly men of the town, whose faces contorted and cackled with laughter. Their worn skin and their tired eyes ached from the years, but Alexius could make anyone laugh; he had the ability to turn back the time for them, and so I did not interrupt. I smiled at my friend, and he smiled back before returning to his theatre. Though he had said no words to me, my heart settled.

I continued my walk beside the river, feeling more at peace, but still caught within the confines of my thoughts. I sat atop a granite boulder; the small white pieces that layered the rifts of the stone sparkled in the sunlight. Interrupting my incessant thinking came a tender voice.

"May I sit?" a woman with blue eyes spoke to me. Her beauty was something to marvel at, though I did not recognize her.

"Please," I responded, though I felt torn because I both craved her attention but I was wary of her beauty.

"You look sad, warrior. What plagues you?"

"That which I cannot explain," I said, the blood rising in my head. My body, at all costs, resisted the urge to open up to her. At once, I understood Achilles.

"Perhaps we might walk, and, if all we find is silence, might we be content with finding such a thing?"

I resisted. "I apologize, lady, d-d-do not think me rude," I stuttered as I left her. The thought of her soft hand wrapped in mine beside the river terrified me. Not now. Not when our gear sat ready, lashed to the ship. Not now, when death loomed on the horizon.

Chrysanthe saw this interaction and walked alongside me as I left the woman. "You will need to let a girl in, Stelios. It shall be your only reprieve from war. Men only understand violence."

"You understand violence," I retorted. She understood it deeply.

She laughed. "Yes, but I also understand love, and peace. And so, because I am a victim of violence, and because it destroyed my life, I also know what Achilles needs. Without me, he might break completely."

She was formidable, she was right, and she was tough.

Weeks later, Leandros and another man wrestled in the arena. Chrysanthe appeared and without a second's hesitation or worry, she confronted the beasts of men who controlled the ring. With confidence she stated to our lion-man, "Your stance is too wide. Your right leg will be swept by any man with the slightest knowledge of combat."

This took him aback. "What would you know about it, woman? A heavy breeze would take you away like pollen, never to be seen again!" The men watching laughed.

Chrysanthe smirked and took off her robe, leaving only the garments that covered her breasts and her undergarments. The men didn't know whether to stare or look away. They looked at the dirt, and the sky, but at the same time her beauty captivated them, so they snuck sideways glances at her figure.

"Let us see how brave you are then, lion-*boy*," she sneered.

At first he was hesitant, but when Leandros charged, Chrysanthe grabbed the underside of his leading left arm and ducked it. In the process she switched her grip of her left hand to her right, and in a flash, she was behind him. She had his back, and she kicked out his right foot, which was positioned far too wide. The giant of a man crashed to the dirt.

His eyes raged. His pride remained beaten in the dirt. The men surrounding the arena cackled like hyenas. Alexius piped up, as he always did.

"By Zeus! Where did you learn that?!"

Chrysanthe put her still perfectly white robe back on. "From my husband." She smiled and turned towards Leandros, who remained shocked and angry.

"Perhaps yours should have taught you the same," she added.

Alexius laughed as if it were the funniest thing he had ever heard in his life. It might well have been.

The following week we prepared to leave for Rhodes. I watched the men assemble their armor before the ships set sail. They pulled the oxhide straps tight to their skin. Their black, shining shields and protections offered a glimpse into how much experience each man had. The older warriors bore battle scars and wounds that not only raised the pink of their skin, but that damaged the perfection of their armor.

Achilles said goodbye to Chrysanthe and the boy, and I noticed the tenderness in which they embraced. I watched how his face changed as he turned away from them. His eyes burned ice blue and his hair gleamed in the sunlight. I saw the determination as they lowered and came to perfect unity with the horizon.

The warrior emerged from inside the man. It was the hardness required for combat.

We sat in the wooden boat together, ready for the long and arduous journey that would unfold before we even set foot on the hostile shore. We met the mercenary group on the southern coast, and sailed the rest of the eastern voyage together to coordinate a joint attack at the Colossus.

Myrmidons. We were deadly and our services cost the lives of many men.

The mercenaries joined us on the coast near the island of Kythnos.

Mercenaries, given the lack of alternatives, were cheap and easy to hire, but fickle and disloyal as they fought for money. Together we made a semi-organized hoard teeming with bloodlust for men we had never met. But they were not the same kind of warriors as we were.

The sea journey was uneventful other than the rendezvous with the mercenaries, whose armor also retained the battle scars of experience but whose faces yearned with desire for blood and coin. Though we sailed in unison, I worried about their nature. I confronted Achilles about my reservations, for fear of stating to the experienced warriors an injustice about a world I did not yet understand.

"Look at their faces, Achilles," I said as our warriors shuffled around the boat, paying little attention to us. "They laugh, but not like us. Their lighthearted nature is malevolent, like a child who has done some untold wrong. But these are not children. They are men, with all the strength of men and the proclivity for violence that men have…"

"But the Myrmidons trust them, or they would not line the beaches as their allies, and so we must have faith too," he retorted.

I was skeptical. "How much trust does one need to thrust a spear in the same direction? What have they proved to us?"

We would soon find out how sinful and depraved these men could be.

"Fret only for yourself and your brother in black," he assured me.

When the legions of Rhodes met us on the beach, they were careless. They had dug into the sand in the early hours of the morning, while the world slept. They hastened when they saw our black sails pierce the horizon. In their haste and their lack of leadership, they dug their long spears into the cold, compact morning sand. We watched them, and because sand had forged us, we waited, as we knew they would die.

The ocean began to warm. Cracks appeared in the drying sand. We feasted as our boat rocked patiently atop the ocean. Our eyes met as we ate, though only briefly. And the handles of our swords dried in the breeze. Above, black sails billowed in the wind. The moments before death were always calm.

The heat gathered strength with each passing minute.

The army of Rhodes watched us with looks of great confusion on their faces, and with anxious glances exchanged between the men. *Why do they not attack?* they wondered. Most of the enemy soldiers stared at the water. We sailed just outside of the range of their archers. A volley of arrows had plopped harmlessly into the ocean hours before.

We conversed little; we said only deep things to one another. Soldiers know when they have a decent chance of dying.

Just before noon, when the sun made its place highest in the sky, I saw the unfolding of the battleground. I made my way to the bow of the ship, unsheathed my sword, and raised it high above my head, so that the rays of sun reflected from its polished and sharp blade. As I did this, the men stirred and looked towards the beach. The now heated sand of the shores began to let loose the shallowly dug pike spears. One by one, the spears hit the sand with a thud.

As the defenses fell and became useless for the protection of the island, a gaze of horror befell the men of Rhodes. My sword, which still remained high in the sky, glistened. I slowly brought the tip of the blade down and pointed it towards the now broken spirits of the enemy.

They knew, in that moment, that it would be the end for them. When the bodies fell, there was no distinguishing them from the lifeless, fallen spears.

In our first war, we took the island. Only one man, a brave soldier of Rhodes, managed to slice a scar on my armor, just above my left lung. Though he knew that the dusk was closing in on him, he still stood and fought. This unsettled me. We had been made to believe that our enemies were evil, vile, and cruel, and yet, his blue eyes held none of these things. He was the same as I, only now dead.

We destroyed them.

In brief time, Krakos' head sat upon a spear under the great Colossus.

His army ran ragged, weakened from his jealously and spite. In his consuming rage, and his unease about his power, he had executed some of his best generals for fear of treason. The officers who remained were the leaders that had been around long enough to promote. These so-called leaders knew little of their land. They were disconnected from both their men and the arduous work that the troops needed to conduct that they did not even understand their own beach.

That is the truth of distrust and authoritarianism in leaders.

Kalliaros spoke to me as we stacked the bodies of the fallen on the shores of Rhodes. A true officer, his palms bore the lukewarm crimson blood of the freshly killed men, and he spoke with conviction and honor and all the guidance that young men search for.

"A leader does his duty; he does not shy away from completing the hard things with the men he leads. He must know and never forget the feeling of returning home with the dirt of his fields underneath his fingernails. Nor must he ever forget the pain that arises in the lower back as a result of dragging the carts. The officer need not spend all his time here — he still has a job to do, an army to organize and train, and he must innovate... And so, he must resign himself to these higher tasks as soon as the feeling of hard, manual labor returns to him. He will then know both of his worlds, the one of the men, and the one of the leaders of men. At this point the officer can lead, and at the same time he will have earned the respect from the men he leads. It is a simple concept, which almost no men follow."

He pointed to the corpses.

"See these bodies, my young friend. Krakos, in his lustful and clouded mind, has rid Rhodes of anyone who appeared to be sympathizing with those lower than him — military or civilian. So, the ones who remained, the leaders that lingered for him, were the ones who gave him the answer he wanted, and not the one he needed.

We do not acquiesce to power — we take it. We do the tough things, the gritty things, with the men we respect the most, to earn that same feeling from them."

He finished stacking the bodies alongside his men and walked to the Aegean to wash his hands of the blood. The salt ran through the wounds on his hands, cracked from battle.

The power of our ranks was in our synchronous spirit. We looked the same, dressed the same, and had undergone the same rigors and adversities. Our men reserved their own identities and personalities, but they harbored their own terrors. Our men — each one different in stature and grace, but relentless in the cauldron of war, and when operating as a team. When unified, we rang a symphony of violence across the battered hillside as a single melody.

But our victory did not prepare us for the level of depravity we encountered after the battle. Enslaved men, women, and children considered enemies of the island state toiled and worked the land in a desperate attempt, not to feed the population, but to survive and to learn unwavering loyalty. In order to keep oppressed citizens in line and under such a rule as this, only the strictest discipline will do.

As we freed the people from their prisons of labor, it struck me how well we knew this feeling. Each person to whom I gave back liberty seemed to lift a small weight from my back.

The men and women stood in line waiting for me to cut their bonds with my sword. One by one I snapped the material and sent them to grab what rations and food we had. A hunched man shuffled along towards me, his wrists chaffed and bled raw from the rope. He looked up at me, and, in a moment of clarity and horror, I saw that it was Nikolai, who had walked the lonely path away from us so long ago. He said no words, but his eyes filled with tears. I patted his shoulder and directed him towards what little comfort we brought.

We found more prisoners. We cut constraints from bleeding wrists all day.

The people of this island had done nothing wrong in their lives except to inherit the unfortunate burden of living on this patch of land, in this moment in time. It was enough for a man to forget the gods altogether, though I also knew that it was a deific amnesia that must have been the cause of this.

Their leaders and conquerors, if you could call them such a thing, had forgotten a crucial element: any man who believed he would need to kneel and present himself to the gods at the culmination of his life, such as I am now, could not possibly act in such a manner. I reassured myself to be steadfast and to not forget the divinity of each individual soul, nor the existence of gods. We won the land because a king who governs based on fear rather than love is an easy target. A society whose discipline stems from fear of their ruler is an easy one to convince. An evil leader is one who exploits his people by taking away everything they hold dear and precious, then murdering those who protest. The men who liberate, as we had been from our tyrant, are unquestionably good. And if only it were so simple, then my life wouldn't have been so painful, and living might have been far easier than dying.

Those who preach their ultimate values and then in turn do not live up to these values and ideas degrade the entire system of leadership.

Men with clear morals reject these types of leaders. This in turn makes the ineffective leader hateful, and angry, and then they harness the full force of evil.

But this is not a story of war; it is a story of the abyss, and how the Myrmidons came to be.

Yes, we took the island. We were superior in our training, our spirit, and our tactics, and we liberated those who sought to be free. If our war was to end at that very moment, we would've been heroic, for all that word means to me now, but that is not the truth. We sent the men to whichever afterlife they believed in, but we were unable to explain exactly why we did so. And though I felt the tides of victory deep within, I also felt the sting of mistake. Who were we to judge? Was it our place to take these things?

As destructive as the tools of war are, steel is inconsequential compared to what soldiers might do in the wake of war. As the blaze of anarchy rises in their blood and clouds their primal minds, they lose their way.

Inside the stone walls of the main city, we saw the worst of it. The mercenaries began to loot the homes. When the citizens resisted, they died. Such cruelty, upon people who needed no more hate.

But what started with the mercenaries soon overflowed to some of the Myrmidons. And it shattered my heart to see the reflection of the flames glinting against black armor. But war changes us all.

It went against every code of ethics we had ever set out for ourselves. The looting grew, and soon rose to torture, then killing, and the burning of the city and its people. Our men stole treasures and lives from the island. They hoarded pieces of Rhodes to bring home, to sell and to feed their families — our salaries were meager. I understood the motivation, the greed, the appeal, but the way they took these things was sickening.

I wanted to drown in the sea to stop the pain.

What then was I to do? Kill those who had protected my brothers and myself? Partake in the horror? Sit and turn my gaze from it? Crying out and suffering were no better.

I did not participate, I could not. But as I left the burning walls of the city I searched for a small corner of the beach, where I would be far enough away from the screaming. I thought about how cowardly I was, and how I had made the wrong decision in coming here, and how I should've died here, at war, not heroically, but just die to rid myself of the guilt. I wanted to die because it was the effortless way out, but when I reached the beach, I saw that I was not alone. Most of the battalion sat on the sand, their eyes focused on the sea and their backs towards the flames that tore the town apart. The demons remained inside the city. These were the men whose ideals drove them away from the chaos, and whose hearts broke knowing that a few of their comrades in black armor were somewhere inside, committing atrocities against innocent people.

Among the innocent of the beach was Achilles.

Together in a group sat Iesos, Deimos, and Teris; the men who had espoused such moral guidelines had at least followed their teachings.

Pyrros was not there. He was among the guilty.

I sought refuge with the only men whom I was comfortable speaking to about these things. At once I understood why the Myrmidons' policy was to keep the mentors with those they've trained.

I knew little of politics.

"How have we fallen so far, in such a short amount of time!?" I raged. "What happened to all we spoke of? We would dare let these men poison our name? Our ethos?! We would dare let them wear the black armor while they defile our codes?"

My chest heaved with anger, and then, as I saw their faces, immediate regret for my outburst filled me.

"Sit down," rumbled Deimos, in the softest tone he could muster. "Menestheus, the leader of Greece, struck a contract with the mercenaries and granted permission for this conduct. He hired the mercenaries to avoid Greek death, to bolster his image in Athens, and to strengthen his ability to call upon the mercenaries again when needed. This is not the first time the Myrmidons have fallen victim to such things, nor do I fear it won't be the last…"

The flames rose from the city. Screams echoed across the beach. The men buried their heads in an attempt to make it stop.

"I blame myself," he continued. "I should have instilled better qualities in your group. I should have been harsher. I should have been harder on men like Pyrros. We thought we could stop this by taking command of the trials, but I see now that this vision was foolish. It is a fine balance, you see, to exploit those qualities of violence when needed, but to also reign them in when they take over — in this, I have failed."

"This makes no sense to me," I added.

Deimos continued, "It is because you are young and naïve. For that, I am jealous of you."

"Why would men think in such terms?" I asked.

"Because the machine of war destroys their souls. They do not pray," Iesos responded.

Deimos continued his explanation.

"If the truth comes out, Menestheus can argue that mercenaries are mindless brutes, have them executed, and lie about any sort of agreement with them. The people will gather and cheer the purity and the morality of their government, while we, the Myrmidons, sail off to distant islands for more death, knowing the truth but being bound by law to keep it to ourselves. And we, the pawns of death, who are made to fight and to die for his fame and support, are then no more ethical than he was, as we had once believed."

Iesos interrupted again. "The truth of war is the evil that hides in all men, and that this evil comes forth not in the most complex times, but at the slightest fracture. In identifying pure evil, one need not look further than one's own reflection. To contribute pure malevolence to the world then you need not to provide vast opportunities to men, but rather the smallest of gaps. Then the orchestrator of this violence can sit back, watch the decay, and revel in the putrefaction. This gives a far better insight to the world, for it is much harder to destroy something small, and yet men find almost every opportunity to do so and to do so in the vilest way."

Teris shook his head. "We almost always do so to the ruin of each other."

"This is my fault," Deimos repeated, stricken with grief.

"Their choices are their own," Iesos stated, both to me and Deimos. "We cannot dictate their failures much as we cannot decree their bravery. The world is a cruel place."

The sounds of riot rose. We felt the abhorrent reverberations upon the very ground on which we stood.

"We cannot stand by while it happens. We cannot do nothing," I responded.

Teris chimed in, "I agree you with, sir, we must put an end to this madness. We must confront them."

Deimos spoke, "Their hearts are gone, friend. They will slaughter you for sport."

Noise flooded the beach, so piercing and thunderous that it felt like the slaughter was taking place inside my head. I fell, shattered by disgust and contempt for my part in this, onto the sand and wept. I shook my head, willing the sickening noises to vacate.

Back on the island and during my trial, I was certain I had journeyed to the depths of Tartarus to face that snake, in that deep abyss. Now that I reflect and I have seen the world for what it is, I remember the dark revolting hell, where I found monsters, but not men, and now I understand why — the villains live among us.

I touched the fresh scar on my armor.

If I thought that my world had shattered, I was unprepared to see what had become of Achilles. When I thought of his youth, I could barely endure the miserable pain in my chest. When I saw him, sitting on the beach, he had changed, and in his eyes, as the tears fell on the sand, came the image of his childhood, of his mother, and all the agony that plagued his exterior, and then, worst of all, he realized the fact that he was now part of them — those who had taken his life away so young.

He exploded with such a rage, such an anger, that he beat the sand with his hands until the blood poured from his fists and the red liquid sank down below the clay. Most of the Myrmidons sat in the sand with us, but none glanced at Achilles. They sat and kicked away the pieces of driftwood near their feet. Achilles looked around. I could do nothing to help him. He clenched his teeth and bloody fists, and there was a rage in him I could not fathom.

But instead of joining us in our cowardice, he acted, and this was where I first understood his godliness.

Acting in the face of evil is divine, while dying, in whatever fashion you prefer, of the soul or of the body, is simple and easy. Instead of resigning himself to his cowardice, he bolted at me, like lighting, for he was quick across the sand. He grabbed me by my cuirass straps, above the chest armor, and he lifted me with the strength of an ox — something he had never possessed before. Just as violently, he dropped so that my feet slammed into the hard earth.

He said only one thing. In fact, he bellowed it, so he would not need to repeat himself to the other dejected warriors.

"Destiny, or history?" he asked.

I needed no further warning, as this succinct mantra had boiled my blood. It was my time to stand for something or become the thing that sickened my heart. In this duality, I found an ease of existence which washed over me like an undercurrent of ocean, a tide that pulls the hearts of men in an unexplainable fashion. It does not move the physical but rather extracts all that which is good and noble. In all the complexities of my internal combat, this leader of men offered to me a binary that cleared my vision. A simplicity that offered an exit. He turned to the other men who had heard his cry.

It was the same Achilles who had barely withstood his training, and who had suffered at the hands of the dominant boys, and who had neared death in his mediocrity, and yet, among all the old and experienced men he was the one most eager to act.

That was the role of Achilles.

In Rhodes, we avoided the halls of hell. Our lives could have been different — easier, and far more destructive.

One by one, Achilles lifted the men up, and as he did, he smacked the hilt of his sword hard into their chests. This rattled both their bones and the very beach upon which they stood. He inducted us into this new regiment of Myrmidons. He was a new leader, who might guide us towards the fields of Elysium.

Teris was on his feet, sword gripped in hand, long before Achilles reached him. The other two needed no aid but they let him pick them up anyways.

As we entered the burning city, wisps of charred and blackened fabric flew far above our heads and made their way to the sea. Achilles, leading from the front, found Pyrros kicking an old man senseless on the hard concrete. The boy we knew as the strongest of us had lost his mind — his rage was unavoidable and immense. We knew then that something had broken in him far before he ever began his training.

As Pyrros turned towards Achilles, the rage in their eyes and the hate they harbored for each other shone through the fire. The flames reached for the sky, and, much akin to their time together on the killing ground during their training, they found themselves engaged in combat. But this time one of them would die.

Achilles ran at him.

Pyrros ducked and slammed his shield into the turned back of Achilles, sending him to the floor. Achilles rose and parried the sword of Pyrros as it ripped towards his neck. Stunned and attempting to control the violent vibration in his weapon from the block, Pyrros took an unexpected step towards the rear.

It was clear in his eyes that he had never experienced retreat before, and he had no clue how to endure it.

Achilles charged.

Pyrros took another step back. His eyes widened with recognition. His hands trembled. His strength meant nothing in the face of true courage.

And he was also met with a different man. Achilles was not the same boy he had beaten within an inch of his life in training. Achilles was not scared because he no longer feared death; he feared weakness above all.

And with each charge, Pyrros' shield blocked the strikes of Achilles' sword. He was losing ground, and his shield dropped lower and lower as he fatigued.

It dropped below the shoulder line. The same one that forged us into men. The same one for which Deimos had sent Achilles to the dirt for in his fight against me.

Achilles ducked a wild swing and landed on his right knee guard. He pivoted and swiveled his body, the metal armor grinding against the concrete as he bowed below the desperate heave of Pyrros' sword. As Achilles rose, he stuck the better part of his sharp edge through the neck of Pyrros, severing the artery and dropping the man to the floor.

And Achilles watched the man bleed to death as was his duty. He listened as Pyrros cried out for those things that would not come to save him.

Some men dub combat "the glorious death" — these men have not seen it up close. They have not had the image burned into them. The heroic heart is that which sleeps beneath the surface. And when I saw death for the first time, when I found myself on the other side of the dark line which divides not only men from different corners of Greece, but of the entire world, I reeled at the calamity of it all. I saw the young, whose spirit matched that of mine, die in agony. I saw old men, who experience outweighed my own, and whose battle-hardened souls had seen much worse than Rhodes, die in the same manner as the young. In the years that followed I searched for the answer as to why some men die in war and some live full lives.

I search for this still, but I now know I shall never find it.

Underneath the moon and in the reflection of the fire of the city, Achilles appeared a different man to us.

"He was granted nothing additional in this moment," said Zeus. *"He merely adopted that which he already created to be. Here, the fingers of the gods ceased to move the pieces of the world. We were fated as spectators."*

Stelios opened his mouth to speak but stopped. It was not the time.

Achilles said nothing as he ripped the sword from the neck of the fallen man. Looking at us with pure iron in his veins, he was not the boy I had met in my youth. Some men saw greatness, but I saw something dark emerge. It was a ruthlessness I could not personally come to terms with. He pointed his sword in the direction of the other men to whom he had deemed unworthy to wear the armor he had earned.

We killed the other warriors; they were no longer a complete unit, but rather singular skiffs drifting in the ocean. They lost themselves in the riot. They didn't even see us coming. But the bodies of our brothers that bled into the sand and the earth still burned my mind, for even in easy victory, and in the most simplistic moral choice, there is still death.

In the grips of this unfair fate, I fought with myself, for evil and good men died together that day, and there seemed no distinguishing them now in death as there was in life. This only proved to me that it was the unraveling of life that corrupted us. In death all of us were equal, and so some men died before they could commit atrocities. Death was then their savior, and they remained pure.

One might argue that the proximity to the end of one's life is in fact the catalyst that drives good people to act in such vile ways. The futility of it all is enough to fracture the strongest mind and to deem one's life meaningless. But then why did I feel such a strong regret towards murdering them, for that's what it was, and why were the others so resolute in their decision to kill their brothers? What drove us to act this way?

And how did we condemn them so quickly, and why, given our training and backgrounds, did some men act as beasts and some not?

It was the dichotomy of all things, and yet it was incomprehensible to me.

For their crimes, we killed them all. We were judge, jury, and violent executioners. In his self-indulgence, our fratricide went unnoticed by each man. They lost themselves in the overwhelming tide of pleasure and violence.

We took their scattered black armor from the blood-soaked earth, because its symbol still meant something to us, and we would not leave it with the dishonored, but rather we would give it back to the sea. The sea could bring it to the places of the earth it felt worthy to judge them.

As we continued through the city, we swarmed across the open market square and tried the save the people, but the pain in the eyes of the liberated bore a hole through me like I had never felt before. We terrified them. Achilles was a monstrous figure during the brutality, but he stayed true to his word. Directing, leading, reassuring — all of these qualities he demonstrated with the utmost professionalism and poise.

When the disorder faded and the fires burned out, we gave the remaining people everything we could as far as food and clothing, and we amassed back on the beach, preparing to sail home and face whatever judgement we had to face for our actions.

Myrmidon flotillas sail in a diamond formation, with the generals' ship at the tip of the spear. As we approached the beach again, our general, Kerberos, huddled the men into a half-moon around him. He had been one of the men on the beach whom Achilles ripped from the ground.

In his rage, my blonde-haired comrade had not even processed who the man was.

"Embark!" the general screamed.

Myrmidons began to board the vessels, and when we all took our places, torches blazing and the spears on our ships pointed for home, we waited for the general's ship to depart.

The order did not come. Kerberos stood atop the bow of his great vessel, which had lions carved into the handrails of ash.

"Achilles! Ship's gallows…" he said, and our hearts dropped. Surely, he would not execute this young man for his actions.

"Sir." A resigned voice resonated from the mass of black armor. Achilles sat next to me, oar already in hand. He dropped it and stood.

The blonde man walked to the front of the small armada, climbed the ladder, and took his place on the hearth of the general's ship. The blood of traitors and mutineers stained the wood of the deck. He did not protest, nor plea. He was at peace with his decision.

Kerberos spoke again, loud enough for the men to hear. "My apologies, young warrior. My memory fails me in old age. Take your rightful place there." He pointed to the general's position of honor on the bow of the ship. "I present to you, men, Achilles. Commander of the Myrmidon forces, general of the black-armored legions. Slave to no man, no king, no god, nor to the tyrant which lurks below."

The now former general turned to Achilles. "Do better than I, my friend."

Kerberos jumped from his ship, and, to my surprise, boarded ours. He sat down next to me, and his old, wrinkled hands picked up the oar Achilles had dropped. My jaw remained open, and he looked deep into my eyes, and said, "You think me old, son? I could pick my teeth in the shine of your fresh armor, and I would use this needle," he slapped my sheathed sword, "to do so. Call me elderly now, son, and I'll out-row you the entire way home."

Three rows ahead, Alexius was shaking with laughter.

But the reality of war is that humor is but a mere escape — we didn't even bring the bodies of our former comrades.

We launched the ships, and we rowed. Achilles collected his thoughts at his place on the ship to my right. I watched his figure cast against the blanket of stars, as he thought long and hard about what his position meant to him. I reflected on what it was we fought for in the first place. The ships moved silently, other than the few murmurs which echoed on the waves, of friends confiding in close friends. In our minds we fought under the veil of morality, and so we went to Rhodes to save its people. But we were mere hammers of the state. Tools which political men exploit. We knew in our hearts we went to Rhodes to enforce the intentions of the government, and not to enforce any sort of maxim we had set for ourselves.

These are not motivations that drive men to die properly. They do not solidify the position of the warrior.

I prayed that Achilles, my new commander, would be able to solve this emptiness I felt inside. He stood atop the lead ship as it cut the waves like a whetted knife.

"Men," he bellowed, as he paced left to right, projecting his voice across the quiet sea. We all stopped rowing. It was silent under the stars.

"I am no orator of great skill or wit. I shall not pretend to be that which I am not."

He paused.

"I am a soldier. My abilities, like all of you who stand here before me and have proven yourselves in countless battles, are in knowing how to kill. I have but a few simple commands for you, soldiers of the night. Look long and hard at your weaknesses..." He fell back on his training, as all soldiers do in the times where they search for character. "Ensure that the man staring back at you from the sea is one whom you can spend the evening with drinking wine, as well as the one whom you can trust in the heat of battle. Ensure this man's ideals align with your own. If we all undertake such journeys, we will win the war."

No philosopher, but he was better than he thought.

"My last command before I leave you be for the voyage is this."

He looked around the men and settled his eyes on me.

"Do not clean your armor," he ordered, as he turned back to the wind.

We were no longer the Myrmidons, those tools of the state who took the spoils of war at the slightest push amid the fracturing of self-discipline. We were the Myrmidons of Achilles, men of honor and code, who disciplined themselves in life as they did in training. That was the start of our lives, and the start of our enduring friction with Greece.

But it was not the end of our pain.

Another warrior gave me leave to rest my arms from rowing. The old man laughed when I accepted, and he rowed harder. Sitting atop the oak of the ship as we drifted home my mentors, Deimos and Teris, spoke in muted tones. I approached them and asked if I might sit with them.

"How are we to continue, my old teachers? How might we still walk the path of the warrior after the actions we took?" I asked.

Deimos paused.

"We must have integrity," he spoke.

Integrity. They beat it into us in training.

Deimos continued, "We must have integrity when courage alone will not suffice. When the enemy swarms like locusts, integrity will see to it that you do not compromise your ethics. These choices are the way of the warrior."

He continued, in that voice which echoes still in the bowels of my mind.

"When men choose the wrong path, the consequences are devastating. In the absence of the choosing to grapple with one's existence, men turn to monsters, and then in turn they derive their pleasure and their power from the destruction of others. Under the crushing weight of life, these men find themselves living without higher purpose. Instead of choice, they search for distraction from the pain, which then results in the pain of the many, instead of the one. We who live brutally are the most fortunate, for in our aggression we remove ourselves from the devastating burden of the world, and because we indebt ourselves to each other we always have purpose. But many men in life do not have such luxuries."

Teris added to this wisdom.

"Men find this sentiment in fatherhood, and also in war — war in the world or the war within. All else fails in the pursuit of morals."

V

CAGES WITH OPEN DOORS

As we sailed the warm ocean back to Thessaly, I watched as the night pulled its curtain over the world, and the stars, bravely passing their horizons, fell into the darkness of the sea to join our hearts. The endless night threw its blanket over us. And still, we knew that the rising of this day's sun would bring with it a gleaming hope for our futures. The consequences of our actions could be death. Sometimes, death is worth it. Or we could face execution by torture, which is just an extended death. We knew also that the Myrmidons were a necessity of the Greek forces — unconventional men in conventional warfare. When we prodded Achilles for answers, he turned towards his men and took a knee, signaling his equality to us.

"We've committed the worst of all deeds. Fratricide, though common in the chaos of war, is punishable by death."

This we knew. Long ago, we had learned it.

"The Greek army needs us. We do not need them, but for orders of war. Let them send the emissaries. Let them send the battle line. Let them send the king for all I care. Whoever challenges us, friend, or foe… We shall slaughter them like cattle. Let those who threaten us with violence remember how violent we are. We will still fight for our nation but not its corrupt politics, for that, least of all, represents us. We will fight, yes, but we will do so on our terms, when we judge the nature of the mission to be worthy. No longer will we function as we have in Rhodes. One wicked act can destroy a lifetime of virtue."

In the vastness of the ocean, we slammed our spears down upon the deck of the boat. The sea itself rippled. The sound travelled through the ship, through the dark water below us and sent a message to each corner of our land. Our violent spears sent each tide of Greece climbing higher upon the far-off sand. We did so cathartically as well, to release those things that had been weighing upon us as we'd sailed. We believed it, and so the sound of our weapons splintering the hard oak beneath our feet was a vicious call to action. Each man attempted to let go of that which haunted him.

It was a message that travelled along the waves and warned all of Greece. We were coming.

Our journey home was not rushed. Frequently, Achilles would stop the ship and with no land in sight, the Myrmidons would swim next to the vessel. Unconcerned with the direction of the gale or the weather, we inhabited a world free from everything. The water below us was crystal clear. A man could see for miles, though he may never see the bottom. The ocean kept us buoyant. Whales breached and sprayed their mist, which landed upon the horizon. Above the waterline the blue sky was indistinguishable from the end of the sea, floating atop a sword's edge in the distance. Below, our legs dangled in the abyss. Achilles and I drifted together. From our skin, the dried blood dispersed.

Achilles and I swam back to the boats and sat among the canvas ropes that hung over the side. Achilles left his feet below the waves, at the ankle line, and let them drift in the warm ocean.

"What shall the way forward be for us now, my old friend?" I asked as he turned towards me, the water falling in beads from the scruff on his chin. He stopped and stared at the dusting of sunrays which now sprinkled the edge of what we could see.

He spoke, "Almost nothing changes in terms of our military preparation. Our trials and our interactions with the town remain the same, but something has to change in the hearts of our men. As soon as their feet brush the wet sand of the beach, this secret stays with us. We rid ourselves of the poison that ran through the veins of our army, but in turn we must stare into the eyes of the wives who we have made widows. We must inform them that their husbands, who they love, died fighting valiantly in battle. We have to watch their children jump from rock to rock, knowing who made them fatherless. And in turn, we cannot scorn their father's image — we will only create more pain. Children foolishly believe that their parent's destiny is also their own."

Zeus spoke, *"Thankfully, young soldier, such things are not true…"*

I agreed with Achilles. "The consequences of life, though the actions we took were moral and rational, are unforeseen and brutal."

When we reached our shores, Achilles, before returning to see his love Chrysanthe, gave me orders to meet the following day at the stronghold of the beach.

"Where our spears line the sand," he said.

Our weapons sat as a reminder and a threat. They were still sharpened. Throughout the day and night, the spears watched the shores with a careful eye. Between the shipwrecks and the dead trees that lined our shores, the spears of the Myrmidons lay ready to make war against any enemy.

Achilles received word that messengers from Menestheus, our king in

Athens, were to arrive the next afternoon.

That evening, I immediately disappeared to seek my refuge in the forest, to come to terms with the things I had done. The dusk passed, and I decided to take a walk to calm my mind. As the moon began to rise, the dust I kicked up rose from my feet to the constellations, taking refuge among the gods. My feet wandered next to the crackling and bubbling of the water. I took a seat upon a smooth but broken boulder and watched the flowing river beneath the stones. I had struggled during our voyage home, with the actions we took, despite their explanations.

A cracking branch ripped me from the depths of my mind. Without thinking, I picked up a jagged rock and prepared.

Swaying blonde hair appeared upon the trail.

"Your nerves are shot, Stelios. What are you hiding?"

"It is our war," I said. "It is not as simple as what we were told long ago." I dropped the stone. "How do we continue from here, Achilles?"

"What we did was justified," he stated.

"That does not make it above condemnation," I replied.

I continued as he sat silent.

"In our haste to rid ourselves of the evil in the men we despised, we broke off a piece of ourselves in the process. It is not enough to hold the soul intact with the glue of decency. Even in the most steadfast rationality there is something that fractures in the destruction of a life. These pieces we shall never get back."

Achilles sighed.

"Each man will deal with this, and each in his own way. War is hell, but it is necessary."

"That was not war, Achilles. It was death, outside of the confines of battle with an enemy. It was self-destruction. And if we continue, we will find ourselves, each time, an increment closer to the thing we set out to destroy in the first place.

"If we do this enough, we will become evil in the process of fighting it. The result is still the same. Our line advanced forward. Our men, we murdered. Yes, they had been vile. They violated the honor we set out for ourselves and the honor of combat. They arrived as devils disguised as heroes. But how do we differ from them now?"

He said nothing, but his face contorted with signs of disagreement.

I persisted.

"Do we not have faults? Do we not fall victim to that which all men do at times?"

"It was not fault, it was weakness," Achilles replied.

"We are all weak in moments," I replied. "Do not consider yourself above such things."

The Myrmidon in the temple paused.

Anger filled his eyes, and he addressed the god.

"Did they plead to you, Zeus, those people of Rhodes? Did they plead their case and explain their considerable sorrows? Did you grant them peace and salvation in the afterlife? I hope with all the longings of my soul that you granted them that at least that. All people deserve it."

"They had no need to beg for salvation, solider." His face turned stern. *"Do not think me heartless. These crimes were not the work of the gods but rather borne from the barbarity of men. I did what I could for them."*

The Myrmidon accepted the god's stern words, but he needed to know more. "And they sit now, peaceful, and with the ones they hold close to their hearts?"

Zeus replied, *"They stroll the meadows where the asphodels sway in the gentle wind. They are at peace."*

"For the first time, certainly," the Myrmidon added, wiping his eye with his tired palm.

Zeus spoke, *"I believe so too, though my heart still suffers for them. Continue."*

I knew the diplomatic talks would be difficult with the Greeks. They reeled with the sting of losing half of their mercenaries. I had little knowledge of governments or their motivations; this kept me happy. But due to my position, as all officers must do, I had to attend the talks the following afternoon.

This was not Athens. This place was ours. Our Greece. We would defend it in a manner that we saw fit. We prepared no seats, nor food. Our armor was not cleaned or polished, as theirs was. We made no attempt to sway the three emissaries from the capital with poise and circumstance. We stood as we were. We represented ourselves as we lived. Our armor was still covered in dried remains, but our skin was clean to show our muscular frames. We were like deranged butchers fresh from the slaughter.

When they arrived, they seemed confident, but this soon faded. The three visitors looked at us uncomfortably. They searched for a place to sit that would not dirty the gold emblems or the fine material that was woven into their uniforms.

We felt in charge. Not in charge because we knew our numbers and our skills were superior, but because we had dragged these men into our world. While we welcomed our primal nature and our smiles grew amongst the dirt and the filth, such things weakened our visitors. Their armor held no scars. The only proof of their worth was the colored merits pinned in rows upon their chests, but we did not know what these ribbons meant, so we did not care.

The men glanced at the dirt, while unflinchingly we took a kneeling pose in the grime. Some of our men took the sand in their palms and rubbed it between their hands. It counteracted the inevitable sweat of a warrior's grasp and allowed the grip on the hilt on his sword to be deadlier. It is not that we were preparing for a fight, but we motioned to the newcomers that we would not avoid one. The sideways glances we received in return meant that they knew there would be no hesitation.

Achilles began the conversation.

"What is your name?" he prodded.

The emissary in black and gold responded. "Bakchos. And yours, Myrmidon?"

He did not answer. "Of whom do you ask? We all are Myrmidon, here." Achilles grabbed a handful of sand the same as we had.

Bakchos smirked. "Whomever is the bravest to speak to. Give us your best warrior, your most cherished soldier, and perhaps we shall converse with him. We did not come here to speak to ignorant boys. Who are you, youth, to question us?" The words snaked from his tongue towards Achilles.

Achilles looked over his shoulder mockingly. "Hmm... Bravest, you say? Most decorated? Most adorned with titles? That is what you Athenians mean when you say 'bravest,' for you know nothing."

The man scoffed at Achilles. "I know nothing, boy? I have seen more battles than you have seen sunsets. See this here?" He pointed to the purple-and-white ribbon upon his chest. "Given to me by Menestheus himself — "

"And you assume, *messenger*, that I tremble upon the sight of men such as you? 'Beware the envoy' — is this the motto of the Athenian armies?"

"I could recount further victories to you, you insolent child, but I'm afraid we must leave before nightfall."

"And yet, I am unworried about a man who demonstrates his proclivity for viciousness. I hold no concern for a man who loudly recounts his victories, either by speech, or symbol." He nodded his head, indicating the ribbons on the uniforms of the visitors again. "Cowards speak in such manners."

The Greek's eyed narrowed. "You dare call me coward, *boy*?"

Achilles drew battle lines in the sand with a piece of driftwood, but his tone turned serious.

"I do not simply dare." He looked up at them.

"My name is Achilles."

He stared coldly at them, eyes filled with venom.

"Watch carefully, *messenger*." Achilles spoke the word with such a degradation of rank that the emissary seethed. "The group of warriors who sit before you entertain no distress for the men standing in the spotlight." He drew a parallel line in the sand with the forgotten wood. He did not look up at the Greeks as he continued, "People are quick to notice these men, and are aware of their actions, but they are no threat. Stop for a moment, and you might see the man in the corner, sitting in the dark. Do you see him?" Achilles asked the man sitting furthest to the left, who had sat silent throughout the engagement.

They sat, scanning the crowd nervously and shifting uncomfortably.

"Hmm. Not yet, I see. I shall provide you further clues.

"One must have the utmost apprehension for this man, for he does not present himself at the earliest moment, nor boast of his aptitude for war. Though his silence bears no explicit danger, beware the man in the corner. Beware. His head bows, but his knuckles are white. He is a monster."

Only the wind resounding off our blackened shields could be heard over the tides from the ancient sea.

"Have you found him, Greek?" Fear crept into the faces of the emissaries. The silence began to wear on them. They listened on the knife's edge of his words.

"This man knows the truth. He is a man with the capacity for violence, who can bring forth the ferocity of the fiend inside him on command. Though, he does so only when it is necessary."

"Show yourself, demon!" The emissary on the right finally burst forth like a broken dam in spring, his head writhing from left to right in desperate pursuit.

Achilles smiled. "Step forth."

The sand cascaded over our sandals as we all in unison moved an inch closer to the Greeks. We gave them just a bit less air to breathe.

"He surrounds you. We are all this man. Choose wisely, what you say to us upon our beach. It forged us. You…" he pointed his piece of driftwood at the men, "…are foreigners."

The Greeks spoke. We were Myrmidons, men not molded from the same clay as they were.

Our Greece was not the same as theirs.

"Menestheus is displeased with your actions."

Achilles answered, his leadership solid but his armor displaying no sign of command. "And he sends his message with what threat?"

"Threat of violence, and of your death."

"You would dare rush the shores of our beaches? This ocean belongs to us. The horizon betrays you."

"And if we rush in the night, where the army of Achilles will fail to see our sails…" he snorted with derision, but his voice wavered. "What slaughter might you face then?" The Greek spoke with anger, though in his fury he lost his advantage. "We outnumber you ten to one."

Achilles leaned in, unflinching.

"We own the night, my friend. Look at my shield and call me a liar."

The Greek sat back. "This unit is important to Greece, and so we are willing to overlook this heinous act, if the Myrmidons pledge to fight in Miletus."

"On the Persian coast? What business would Athens have there?"

"Our capital runs short of iron. Miletus has uncovered ore in the mountains, and they have refused the request of Menestheus."

"Why?"

The Greeks grew impatient.

"It matters not *why*, Achilles. To refuse is a refusal of the state. It is an incompetence in leadership, and it is disloyal in the most offensive way. We do not refuse the requests of Athens, and you have much to learn of diplomacy."

"I have much to learn of diplomacy but little to learn of men, and so, I refuse this combat and the commitment of my men."

His insolence stunned the visitors.

But Achilles gave no sign of backing down.

"The Myrmidons will no longer take part in the whims of politicians. We will not resign ourselves to anything less than the honor of combat. We will not kill for the economic wants of the state. If we continue down this road, we will descend again, as we have before, and this is unacceptable to our brothers and us. Do not make the mistake of asking us for this."

"To your demise, you refuse Menestheus. You will bring death to your comrades."

The Greek's threat echoed into the silence of the beach.

Achilles looked hard into the eyes of the men. He looked at them as he had looked at me on that beach in Rhodes, with unyielding force and strength of character.

"Prove it." His menacing tone rang out like the steel of his sword. "The blood still dries on the stones of Rhodes, from men who thought they were superior to us."

A hushed tension filled the air.

The diplomatic conversations had ended.

As the Greeks sailed away, I stayed behind and sat on the shores of the starry ocean. Hours before, the sun had dipped over the crest of the endless sea. The earth swayed and the sky moved and caught between them my body remained. All around us the world moved. Everything shifted except our feet, our bodies, and our ideals about the greater future that we had carved for ourselves.

Achilles approached me, keen to speak of the day's events. The dismissal of the emissaries caused me considerable apprehension. Achilles and I both knew that if the Greek army did decide to try us for our crimes, our bodies and the bodies of our comrades would, in short order, be swinging from the cypress trees, whose limbs remained light enough to sway but sturdy enough to hold our corpses as the blood drained into the earth.

"Must we dismiss them so hastily? I am with you, do not mistake the meaning of my inquiry, but even we need allies. We've made this small corner for our men, in such a wide and immoral world, and though our purpose appears fulfilled, there is an insignificancy that I cannot shake from my bones. We have to be careful."

"Stelios, you think me unwise?"

"You speak from the heart, which is the most admirable part of you as a leader, but the heart is deceptive as well, and when it rushes blood to your veins, you act on emotion rather than a consideration for all the factors of the situation."

He turned towards me, his eyes narrowing with each word. "You would make a better commander?" he threatened.

"No," I said, "I am merely doing what a good captain does: I am giving to you the unaltered truth. How you deal with that truth defines you. Look at yourself now; the sinews in your arms flex. You let the emotions get the better of you back there, and I do not blame you. Those men are no more useful than the scum that collects below old boats in the harbor. But Achilles, old friend, we cannot enforce an ethos from a place of exile. We cannot enact moral difference if we have no battle to fight."

He nodded, the furious blood slowly draining from his cheeks. "I hate them. All of them. I value you, Stelios, but your ideals have no place in this world. My mother thought the same things about men and war."

Though it hurt hearing these words from a man I'd known as a boy, I understood him. Underneath the stoic exterior, the battle scars, the wounds, and the black of Achilles' armor was the pain of emptiness. Even if we could embrace the politics of the state, what good were we, those who acted only as whitecaps act upon the waves of the world, who kill, and die, in the pursuit of something we estimated did not exist? We acted on faith regardless, but faith alone. He simply acted upon what he knew — hurt.

"I wish that in our moment, this moment we share together, Achilles… I wish only that the gods would send us a sign, an image manifested in the clouds, something that might reinforce our commitment, the direction our lives have taken. I pray to Zeus for my soul to settle. Does your heart not wish for the same, brother?"

Achilles shook his head and looked down. "A winter surrounds it."

"The severity of which you choose, Achilles."

I skipped a rock onto the crystal-blue sea, which slapped the water on its broad side three times before drifting beneath the surface.

"What would you have me do then, Stelios?" His blonde hair rustled in the wind. His anger flared once more.

"Take the concepts we were given. The codes which Deimos, Teris, and Iesos taught us. But do not rely solely on the words spoken to us as our truth. If we only listen and never speak, or if we only speak and never listen, we will suffer the consequences of villainy, which will destroy us. Granted to us were foundations through training for war, yes, but not pure guidelines for how to live a good life. Without the grandeur of nature, as here in the presence of the ocean," I kneeled down, my fingertips gently breaching the surface of the cold sea, "we cannot reflect —— we view ourselves only as soldiers."

Achilles disagreed. "We take what we need through blood and steel, Stelios. Forget the ideals and follow the rules we now understand — it is only strength that conquers."

Again, I fought back, "No man wants his guidelines to be so comprehensive and total that his entire existence is dictated, for there is no courage in existing this way. In balance there is peace."

Achilles kicked the sand in anger. "In war, only blood speaks! Balance your triumphs and tragedies, friend, but earn your victory *only* through conflict. You forget who we are. We are but beasts bound for guts and glory. Do not philosophize, and do not ponder. Or do, and let it destroy you. I do not care, but I will not follow you down that path."

He began to walk away from me, leaving me alone.

I shook my head and called out to him. "Then we will die as brutes, far before our hearts cease."

He stopped hard and looked back. "And you will thank me for the death of your soul, for it will be your soul, and not your corpse, which rots in the sand."

Achilles addressed the men the next morning. "No more will the

Myrmidons allow men to abandon their brothers. Contracts will be issued. Terms will be agreed to. We are warriors, and we shall act like it. Any Myrmidon who is found to have abandoned his post before his time is served will be guilty of treason." This fired the hearts of the young men — they believed harshness to be the key. But Kalliaros and the older warriors looked worried. Achilles looked at me with no acknowledgement whatsoever for what we spoke of the day previous. I shook my head and walked away from the group.

I asked the gods to guide his path. The wind had died down in the night.

Zeus nodded at the Myrmidon as the small warrior looked up to the great god. His voice boomed through the chamber, *"Though the gods may try to act holy, we fall victim to the same transgressions of men. We cannot provide the path. We know it not ourselves…"*

"How then, God of Thunder…" the Myrmidon asked, with the utmost deference, "does a man reflect on his life, even in incredible success, and find it to be a worthy endeavor? In the gaps that governed our beliefs, how does a man must use these concepts to reflect and define his own morals? If he should choose the nihilistic path, if he condemns his belief systems completely, his life turns to horror. And even if he chooses the right one, he falls into conflict with his comrades. Even in the most affluent and stable men, the decay of inner strength eats away at them. I was lucky in a way. I was not in danger from the unexpected, but from the voluntary. This distinction triggers a different part of the mind. To find oneself in the blaze of chaos matters only if one chooses to put themselves there. This is the only method of courage that does not rely on chance, and by definition the only true courage.

Zeus spoke, *"True courage. Such a thing I have only seen a number of times in my eternal life. The Myrmidons brought this courage forth, did they not? Some, yet not all?"*

Sadness gripped the humble soldier. "Not all, Zeus. And courage is the father of all virtues. Without it, we cannot face the world."

Returning to my humble home that night I racked my armor on the wooden stand in the corner of my room. The countryside was peaceful, and the moonlight, in beams, broke the dark clouds above my home. Sailors believe in the power of the clouds, in their ability to foresee the future. They put their trust in the power of the gods and they, as I did that night, watched these prophecies from the peaceful countryside.

I believed the rolling hills were only peaceful because they were absent of us. In the quiet of the evening, I watched as the torches diminished in the far-off towns. I listened to the animals in the distance. Mostly I prayed for peace. But how could we earn peace? Prayers are not answered in such a way. And following my prayers that night, as I did each evening, I sharpened my sword with the smooth stones given to me by my mentors, such a long time ago. When I realized no answers would come to me, I knew I needed to ground myself in the world again.

It is for this purpose that movement is key. It removes us from pain by inciting pain itself. It is the cold, or the heat, the agony that drives our legs upon the mountain, the aching of our shoulders from the swings of our swords, and the blistering of our hands upon the sharpening stone; we have no choice but to remember that we are alive.

Our fragility is our reminder of our mortality. Our pain is our gift.

And sharpening the sword is a balanced skill.

Strap the leather too loosely, the handle of the sword may slip. Strap it too tight and the wrap may break. The sword retains some stability in either case, and a man can still use it to kill — though, he risks some loss of precision.

Next comes the oil. The oil keeps the rust away. A soldier strives for balance, but overuse or underuse can both have adverse outcomes. With each step done incorrectly, the soldier compounds his disadvantage.

We manage these things in war.

The sharpening of the metal — this is the key.

At first, I found the pressure of the stone to be too great, which resulted in the ruin of the edge of the blade. I was young then. When my pressure was too low, or if my stone held some unnoticed imperfection, the blade did not cut through bone. My hands ached when I found this to be the issue.

It is also no mistake that the blade, while being the most nuanced and fragile thing I sharpened, was also the most powerful. This is not only true in war, but in life, in that our decisions and our ability to master the finest points result in the greatest impacts. And, as it is with all things, I could not master this skill without first failing miserably in its pursuit, for a man cannot master that which he has not attempted or that which he has attempted but without the full commitment of his being.

When we met the next morning, Achilles looked weary, as if fresh from battle. In leadership, he suffered from the same ailment that all leaders do — the reflection of decision, the requirement to confront one's decisions. We knew he meant to reinvent our army, not by its hierarchy or positions, but rather for its tactical and strategic goals to align with its character and morals. But there was anger within him. A lust for revenge reared its head. His mother's image burned into him, and though I trusted the man, vengeance is the greatest of all evils. It has no end. Where there is violence, there shall always be revenge. Upon his shoulders sat a fine balance, from which Achilles could either find our demise or our greatness.

Though we would not be murderous tools of the state, we could not fully run from its influence either. Life pulled us in different directions, and so we struggled to find the proper balance that might have allowed us to be good men. Some of us faltered. Evil beckoned to some of the men I once knew, and to those it found, it consumed.

VI

THE COSTS OF WAR

Months passed, and the air wrapped its cold fingers around us. Achilles rejected multiple summonses from the Greek politicians, for they held no convictions of good will and demonstrated only the wants of the economic and tyrannical power that Menestheus craved. Achilles knew that we could not hold out forever — a soldier's income is related to his ability and willingness to fight. The Greeks became impatient with our actions. Our men became impatient with the lack of war. Achilles bolstered the amount of time we spent in the training complex to give the men the chaos they craved. But even that created problems. Leandros, having already defeated the man he sparred with, lost his temper, and broke the man's leg with his wooden shield. The crack was that of the limb of a cypress tree in a heavy gale. The soldiers' bloodlust, the rage in their eyes, was something I knew all too well. But I started to fear it as much as crave it.

Kalliaros approached me one afternoon after battle drills to discuss the conflict brewing in the land of the pharaohs, to the south.

"Egypt calls, my friend."

"What business have we there?" I spoke.

"War is our business. Look at the men, they hunger to put to use that which they have trained their whole lives for. Deny them this and the cracks will grow."

"But what validations are there?"

"Take your pick. Money. Glory. Allies. Traitors. There are always justifications if you look deep enough."

He was right. The only lines that divide soldiers from politicians are the ones etched upon their shields. Morality is relative. War is inevitable.

"To Egypt then," I agreed.

Achilles decided that Kalliaros should take a small battalion to North Egypt. I would be second officer in command to him. The infantry units of Argos, to the south, were already engaged in a long-standing war with the forces of the pharaoh, and soldiers kept dying.

This pleased Menestheus, as Achilles finally acquiesced to a wartime commitment from the Myrmidons. And Achilles, despite his best intentions, could not operate completely outside of the Greek hierarchy. He was also a man of combat — a soldier who could not find himself nor know who he was outside of carnage. What started with good intentions in Rhodes disappeared with the war in Egypt; we went to war not because we believed the cause, but because it was there, it would always be there, and because we knew nothing about ourselves as men without it. I found out that any ideals I still had simply bent under the pressure to exist in the world. So, I left for a war that was far from my heart and my bed to prepare for a conflict I didn't believe in.

I asked Kalliaros for one favor. "Let me bring Alexius."

"Is he not part of the third battalion?"

"He is, but he brings something to war we cannot lash to the boats."

We had heard of the horrific slavery that was commonplace in the Kingdom of the Sun, and so we used that as our moral justification. Menestheus wanted Egypt for its rank in the world, for its great pyramids, and for control of the massive shipping lanes of the Nile. He who controls this river controls the entire trade route of the Southern Sea.

We ignored all of those things because soldiers need to ignore them.

"How quickly we forget what it does to us," I said to Deimos as we packed the ships.

"Soldiers always die in war, sir," he responded.

I turned to him. "Not dying. Killing."

"Ask the gods then why we love it so," Deimos growled.

"I do not love it. But if I get the chance, I shall ask them, old friend. I shall ask them why Myrmidons crave it, even when the sun rises over our places of happiness."

"Men of violence miss it merely because nothing in life compares. Nothing is as complex as the tactics or strategies of combat, and yet nothing is as simple — kill, or perish. Soldiers love it because it no other arena in life presents them such loyal friends. Nowhere else do they find themselves relying on their brothers to save them. And, when fire rises, the men they love as siblings continuously validate this bond by demonstrating that, even if it should cost them their lives, they shall not desert their teammates. Tell me, Myrmidon, have you ever found such sentiments outside the crucible of war?"

"I cannot say I have. I found something else… but it was different in every respect… She was the dawn rising… She was everything that conflict was not…"

Zeus nodded his head. *"I know."*

Stelios could muster no words, and he would not allow his voice to shake before Zeus. With every muscle, he held firm, as he had always been taught to. Breathing deep, he pushed all of that down below. But even when a man buries his sorrows, he must still one day visit the graveyard.

The Myrmidon clenched his fists and cleared his throat. He steeled himself, and then he resumed his story.

Our route took us down the eastern coast of the Greek kingdoms. We sailed past the tip of Euboea, between the islands of Andros and Ceos, where the water was lucent, and the wreckage of ships so shallow that a man could touch the antique graves with the tip of a long spear. Men had waged primeval wars there. Their bodies slept in wet, cold graves that haunted the crystal sea. They were men like us, from time long past. We continued past Aegina, and the Peloponnesian landfall, past Sparta, home of great warriors and ash trees bent from the strong southern winds. We passed through the gap between the islands of Cythera before we hit the western shores of Crete. We felt the heat of the sun there — a far stronger sun god than what we knew in the north. And as we continued along our quiet journey, we spotted Mount Ida, far in the distance.

The summit remained hidden above the sky. The ship pitched as I grasped the woven rope, leaning my body out across the skimming, clear water of the sea. Kalliaros watched as I stretched out my fingers, hoping to get as close as I could to the cracked snow crests which lined the peaks of Ida. In my mind I could picture the sting of the ice on my fingertips. The hot sun burned my skin as it reflected from the waves that broke from the bow. I could imagine the cold of the mountain on my palms. The ridges of the sacred mountain, which lay just below the summit barely broke the ring of clouds, but it appeared as a hallowed place to me, and tall. Kalliaros spoke to me of its importance. "Home of Rhea, Titaness and Daughter of the Earth."

"And from my limited knowledge of the gods, it is a place which weighs heavy on your heart, Zeus. It weighs heavy on mine as well."

Zeus looked towards the windows of the hall, searching for the horizon. *"I remember it well. It is where I sowed the fields of my youth. It is where I learned the pains of family, and how even horrific men can father young children. Within the mountain I contended with those things we spoke of. They are always near to my thoughts, even now."*

I wished to stop, but Egypt lay close. We pressed forward. We made landfall within a half-moon bay, where the rocky cliffs mixed with the inlet. A massive military effort was already in full motion. The water was not the deep blue of home, but turquoise, having been boiled for much longer by the ages of the sun. The sand, while similar to home, lay peppered with black pebbles, instead of the white ivory of Thessaly. The sand was more menacing to my gaze, and when I bent down to pick up a handful of the mixture it scalded my hands. This was not a place we knew, though it appeared very close to the same. We needed to be careful of its deceit.

We had not arrived to a melody of peace. The sounds of combat raged in the distance. Pristine swords clashed. Bellowed orders rang across the land. Courageous charges echoed across the black sand and clanged their tune off my shield. We needed to move. I knew the sounds of dying men. I had heard it too many times in my life.

Kalliaros heard it too. His face changed from the same curiosity. In his hands he also held a burning handful of the peculiar sand, but he did not drop it. The sounds of madness grew louder.

The four sons of Eos had changed the direction of the wind, and now like a stream of parasites the dust from the battle latched onto our bodies. Burrowing and digging its teeth into the pores of our skin it became a part of us. Upon our shoulders we accepted the earsplitting noises of death. A squall brought the smog of decay — the haze that rises from the battlefield, which, for men who are not engulfed in the inferno, turns their stomachs to acid.

Only the men who had felt death's touch looming over them kept their dinners down. And it was common to find, back at the camps, the attendants, the men who manned the logistical side of combat, enveloped in full fits of vomiting.

Kalliaros directed his men, demanding that in that moment they listened only to their courage and grit. His features hardened and his eyebrows lowered. He transformed, upon hearing the sights and sounds of combat, from tourist to a leader of warriors.

"Drop, drop, drop!" And we threw all our nonessential gear to the side.

"Battle lines — to hill base!" Allies fell by the second.

Battle lines assembled, I found myself in the center of my unit of twenty, relaying orders from Kalliaros but given autonomy to control my unit if there were any breaks in the line. Alexius was in the front left of my contingent, ready to bring violence to the enemy.

We crested the hill. The Egyptian land shifted underneath our feet, in waves. This was new to us, and dangerous. The sand and the shifting tides of war were our mentors from long ago, but we could not speak to this earth.

The Egyptians stood atop the next set of dunes, not far from where the ocean met the sand, and where our boats had carved their place into this foreign land. Surges of Egyptians battled with our brothers from Argos. Our allies wore high-plumed helmets lined with black vulture feathers. The Egyptians wore white linen and bronze. Waves of carnage tore across the ancient sand sea. Bodies lay strewn about the battleground. Pieces of what was once flesh and bone now sat motionless in a sea of chaos.

The Egyptians fought in rows twenty men wide, forty men deep, with long pike spears and short crescent-shaped battleaxes for close combat. Their skin was darker than ours. The men looked fierce. They were an ancient people who worshipped the sun, and their bodies showed their piety. But our black armor stole from their gods. We realized as we engaged them that the more ferocious they appeared, the more cowardly they fought.

But their contingent of Medjay frightened me. They were the Egyptian elite — our brothers, who on a different, peaceful day we might have embraced as equals and learned from. These men, whose hair was all cressed in a comparable way, were only fitted with loincloths and a *khopesh*. They sat in the back of the line, waiting. But the conventional armies of Egypt were not in complete disarray as the men of Rhodes had been. They had seen war before, and so they knew its consequences.

Our men reveled and cheered at finding themselves in the crucible of combat again. They frothed at the mouth for blood. And I admit, in the violence I also found some meaning again.

Kalliaros told me once, "War is not complex. The best officers take the complexity of war and strip it down to simple commands. Move. Cover. Left flank. Right flank. Combine these objectives with the talents and aggression of our ranks and the enemy shall find himself overrun with a tactically superior foe."

Though soldiers, the Egyptians, having spent their time reaching for the sky had forgotten the knowledge of the ground. Their pharaohs had subjected their slaves into becoming little more than an angry hoard, a workforce who toiled in the hopes that their selfish leader would meet the heavens. Their leaders forgot the earth they grew up on, and when they charged at us, they did so in one extended line. Their lines bent. Their formations swayed and lacked discipline. We Myrmidons split the battalions into rectangles, with the long edge perpendicular to combat.

The front of our unit appeared narrow to the Egyptians, and deep. When we charged them, and we encountered the rough terrain, we were not torn like old fabric as they were. The Egyptians forgot their own land — there is no more disloyal thing. Their battalions frayed, and their commanders scattered. In the chaos and volume of war, a warrior can only hear that commander who he has listened to throughout the chaos of training. When these men found themselves hearing the distant and disordered commands of these men, they could not comprehend them, their lives ceased.

The black swarms of our ranks ripped the hillside to pieces, and in our unity, I found that the eternal verity of our lives was that the simple act of acting bravely meant much more than that. I saw the physical limits of our capability drift away like the fall leaves from the trees.

In the Myrmidons, I saw only courage.

But in the eyes of the Egyptians, I saw two sentiments — fear and envy.

In our rage and our devastation, we created a creed which all men not only feared but coveted. Not only did they fear our decisive fury, but in a complex way they sought our approval, as if in a different life we might have worn the same armor. When we came flying at them in battle like angry brutes, they knew not whether to strike us down, or beg for our acceptance.

The battle ceased for the night. We had devastated their ranks, but we had gained little ground — war is usually this way. I often wondered how many bodies we sacrificed for how many handfuls of dirt. Each soldier took the evening to pray to whatever gods they believed in, to collect their dead, and to eat, perhaps for the last time, a meal with their friends. I watched the smoke of their fires as they cooked their meat. Under the Egyptian canvas of the heavens, the smoke from our flames mixed with the smoke from theirs. Indistinguishable as they met in the sky, the smoke disappeared into the beauty of the darkness above. The stars took the same positions in the sky as they did in Greece. The sun set in the same place in Egypt as it did from my bedroom window back home.

Deimos saw conflict brewing in my eyes. He was, despite his aggression, a keen observer of men. He sat down next to me, upon a great boulder, ancient to the land and which had seen countless pharaohs and wars. "Sir…" It still took me a moment to realize he was speaking to me.

"We do not take it into consideration — our similarities." He motioned to the smoke from their camp.

I responded, "Who are we to judge such things? These men live similar lives to us. Their wives and children miss them as they make war; their families grieve for them in death, in whatever form their ritual takes. Only the director changes."

"Even still. Such is war and life." Though we had spoken as equals for so long, it still threw me. I would never forget that once, long ago, this man was my teacher — the devil of my nightmares. But I understood him more deeply now. He needed to train warriors. Despite his personal ideals, the man knew that I would be making the choices that may lead to his death, or his victory. He conducted himself in training as a demon, but in war as a hero — this was a demonstration of the utmost professionalism. Deep down he knew it was necessary to shut everything out except what the moment required. I needed to harness his practice of war, or I would get my men killed, and a different kind of dishonor would plague me. I needed to apply his approach to war, but a demon I was not.

The next morning, we took the fight to the enemy, like nothing I had ever seen before.

We overran them and they, in their hearts, thought that the night had fallen, and that they had been fighting all day long.

A desperate body slammed into my shield; I stood my ground. With a heave I lifted the edge of the black shield upwards and felt the shattering of an Egyptian jaw. From his mouth the blood flowed, and his teeth shattered in small pieces across the abyss of my armor. With a lunge he tried to live. With a thrust I ordered him to die. And his god was still high in the sky, but my armor brought to him the dusk.

As the battle ceased again that evening, we collected the dead. Those of us who had fallen, and who had been lucky enough to die a hero's death, were now gone. We grieved, but we also reflected upon our own fate. We had chosen the right place and moment for our survival, despite how unconscious these choices were.

Alexius summed it up as we burned Nikephoros.

"We chose the right moment to strike and to rain destruction on the foe, and at the same time we chose to hold up our shields up at the exact time when death might have been brought unto us. And yet in my heart, I do not feel like we are the lucky ones."

"Nor do I," I responded as the heat of the funeral dried the tears from my eyes.

Only in battle did I begin to understand the makings of men.

The second day was much as the first, but hidden throughout the satisfied beasts of the Myrmidons, a toxin seeped.

I saw fissures in the men, Myrmidon and Greek alike. While the Argive attendants cooked the bread and heated the oil in the steel pans, too many men sat apart from their brothers. Too many men stared for too long at the surface of the earth — the gravel and soil that was not their home. It is easy to be brave in chaos, but, like in the tent we all shared as boys in training, silence diseased the soldiers.

The soldier paused and spoke to Zeus, "In war, it is the silence between the movements of mortality that matters most."

"Such movements I shall never know," said Zeus. As the divine voice echoed throughout the chamber, the soldier realized that even gods could harbor regret.

I searched for Alexius after supper, whose silence never had a chance to flourish. He was laughing. He had a quality about him that healed soldiers tired of death. Three men of Argos sat around him; these soldiers I recognized only from milling around the camps.

Alexius was telling jokes about the Egyptians. The men howled with laughter and before I had even heard the details I smiled. Alexius announced my presence as if I were the pharaoh himself.

"Brave and wise leader!" he shouted, waving his hands in the air as if casting some unseen spell. "Dost though mind joining us?"

I shook my head, laughing. In my position I was stuck. Answer the clown and he ridiculed you further; don't, and he called you weak and ridiculed you just as mercilessly.

"The greatest officer of the Myrmidons is a mute, I see! Tell me, sire," he bowed sarcastically, "do you mime battle commands, or do you utilize a guttural sound, from the stomach, like a mighty brown bear who finds his mate in the grips of passion!"

I had no words. I continued to smile and shake my head at this buffoon.

"I tell you men, should we not defeat the Egyptians tomorrow, do not allow it to trouble you. Our officer here shall see to it that the battle is won. By Zeus, I swear, each one of their men shall expire through old age, before he ever utters a syllable!"

We all chuckled, if only for quick respite.

One of the Argives spoke up. His beard was black and layered with grey, and his eyes were green, close to the shade of the sea upon which we had landed. "Who knew that the Myrmidons had such a developed sense of humor!" He laughed. "We were always told you were savage beasts, devoid of pain or laughter from ingesting too many poisons!"

I smiled. "Well, to be honest," I nodded at Alexius, "I think this one accidentally received an extra dose or two."

Soldiers need these breaks. It was our constant proximity to the vicious temperament of the world that brought forth our laughter.

Alexius and I walked the shoreline that evening, and despite his now solidified position as brigade fool, he had a deep soul, and he thought about what he said, especially to me.

"The sun sets, Stelios. Tomorrow the stage shall once again be set for us. The Egyptians are no joke. I caught a scimitar on the left greave the first morning, just above the ankle, and I can barely walk today." He pointed to his leg. "Yet another scar," he said.

I agreed. "And yet you ridicule the men we killed today. How do you find these things so easy to do, having been so close to death?"

"How can we not, sir?"

"Do not call me sir in this moment."

He paused.

"I must fall back upon humor, to cleanse myself of the days past."

"It is a gift you own, my friend."

"And one of the only gifts I can provide in those moments," he added. "But I saw you today. Your eyes focused upon the enemy. Your orders were clear and concise. Men live because of you. That is your gift."

"And yet, I dread the night. For when all of them are fast asleep save the sentries, and the embers from the fire glow orange from the black ashes, I do not rest. My legs grow weak and collapse, as they have done in all our wars previous. My hands shake, and my chest heaves with sadness, crushed by responsibility. It is as if a demon approaches me and takes the world from me. It happens only briefly, for a moment, but what terrifies me is for the men to witness such weakness. They would lose all respect for me."

He looked me deep in the eyes, a friend, and warrior. "No man will ever lose respect for you. For you to think this is madness. Each man who lays his head down on the sand tonight respects you more than you know. Not once have you shifted blame to your men. Not once have you asked your soldiers to take an action you yourself would not have the courage to take. Not once have you taken credit for the work of others, and even when the recognition was yours to take, you did not accept it. A leader is not someone who lifts the heaviest stone or who takes the most lives in battle. He is not defined by numbers, nor physicality, nor ruthlessness. His care for others defines him. These men," he indicated to the sleeping soldiers, "would sail through the narrows of Hades with you because they know that if you asked them to do so, you would be holding the oars."

"I only did that which felt natural," I said. "Nothing more."

"And that is where you have won." He pulled a sack of wine from his gear, forbidden until the culmination of battle. "Let us drink, and toast to living long lives as friends, and sitting as old men on the banks of the Pineios together. We, who bled the most, and slept the least."

He took a swig and held the prohibited wine towards me.

"How did you smuggle this here?" I asked.

"That is Argive wine, my friend, looted from the stores of our allies myself; that is why it tastes so sweet."

"Because it's Argive?" I asked.

"Because it's stolen."

"To peace then," I replied, "if we both find it after a lifetime of violence." I drank the wine. It was sour and warm, and the bubbles crackled on my tongue.

He laughed. "The officer drinks! There is no way I can be reprimanded now, for I shall drag you down with me, my friend."

"You overestimate my rank, Alexius. The commander would tie us to a tree and whip us both with pleasure," I laughed.

Those who seek only the comforts of life will never know what that moment meant to us. This sensation is unattainable. War brings to the forefront all that is insignificant. The opposite is true for those who seek only vengeance and retaliation. For men, revenge is patting the blaze with dried brush from the summer fields. It burns with intensity, but it does not last — the hearts of men act like fire. Without contrast our lives are meaningless. Our hatred, our love, and our passion are but simple emotions, bound to fall away with the ruthlessness of time and the short memories of mankind.

But bravery — the ability to laugh when tomorrow you may die — is the fuel that lasts. Bravery is the act of continuing. It is the act of moving the feet, of forcing the muscles to contract, of moving towards the sound of chaos, instead of away from it. Bravery exists on both sides of the divide that runs through every soldier's heart, and it is the fuel that feeds the fire for the longest amount of time.

Teris once said to me a simple phrase that I will never forget.

"Be brave. Discard all of those things which are ignoble."

And because we stood in those moments and faced the danger, we will live forever.

But even with all the bravery I found on the Egyptian coast, there was a moment that ripped my stomach from my midsection and hammered it into the dirt. In the weeks that followed, it brought me to unfathomable depths of grief.

The morning after Alexius and I spoke, the battalion fought a hard fight. The men were stunning to watch.

A small group of the Egyptian Medjay broke the left of our line, and despite all of my tactical awareness, clear commands, and prudence, I lost concentration. For only a split second the curvature of the battlefield escaped me, and it cost me everything. The Egyptians slammed the left line of the Myrmidons. The elite force was, at the same time, flanking hard right, using the sand dune to corral and enclose my unit. I saw what was to happen, but too late. Soon, my soldiers would be completely encircled by the warriors of the sun, and we would lose the entire unit. I roared a command. "Press back! Full line!" But Alexius saw the issue before I did and acted to correct my wrongdoing.

He saw that if the leading Medjays broke the line, they would destroy the soldiers of the Argives on the weak side and have them pinned. This threatened the entire battle order, and all of the allied men. The battle itself rested on this loss.

I should not have pulled the line back, and to stay and to hold the line alone meant certain death. But my dear friend, whose humor was only outweighed by his courage, did not turn his back. He did not run as I had ordered. Rather, his sandals dug into the sand, his grip tightened on the hilt of his weapon, and in turn, he saved all our lives.

I saw the recognition in his eyes. It was not fear, but rather that of a man who saw death coming for him — a death I caused. He knew this, and still he fought three of the Medjays at a time. Sparks from their swords danced in the hot sun. He blocked a lunge from a *khopesh*, but too many weapons bore down upon him, and I heard the unmistakable sound of steel as it ripped through flesh. He paused, and for a minute I thought he would falter. He did not. He picked up a rogue helmet and slammed it across the face of his enemy. And, with all the bravery of a Myrmidon who feels the icy fingers of death upon his neck, he steeled himself for the next attack.

I tried to save him. I pushed and shoved and climbed my way through the sea of bodies. My arms were almost completely useless in the chaos, caught between the indistinguishable corpses of the living and the dead. I willed the sand to move me towards him, but I received no response from the earth. There was little room at all to maneuver. My heart pounded with desperation and fear. Slamming the hilt of my sword into an Egyptian helmet, I broke through the swarming ocean of death. I freed myself, but in the final moment when I thought there might still be some hope to save him, our eyes met for the last time in that life.

Before the tide of war took him away, my world paused for a moment. All sound subsided. Each noise of war silenced, as if I'd collapsed, sinking far below the sea. And in the quiet, he said to me, smiling, "Bring my wine to the Isles, my friend."

The next noises were deafening.

His body lay lifeless in a sea of chaos. His comrades, realizing his valor and the tactical situation, returned to hold the line. They drove the enemy back, spurred by his heroism. The next few hours we fought like animals, and I pushed the searing pain of my heart far below the surface. Each confrontation was a blur. I have no recollection of the rest of the days' war. It was too much for me to bear.

When the battle died down, I approached his body. I never let my men see me weep. But I see him even now. Vividly. As if in the light of the day. He was handsome and gritty, which made his mangled image even harder for me to accept. His once sharp chin and expressive eyebrows were little more than cut flesh and bone, and though I was present in the moment of his death, it shook me to the core. An Egyptian bronze-tipped shield had smashed the beauty and laughter from his face, and the weapon, still enveloped with the blood of my friend, lay face up in the sand. The sun cooked the matted blood into a brown mixture, like sugar. What a man he was. What a Myrmidon, a soldier, who discarded the pains of his youth to build himself into a demon of war. What a waste of a beautiful life. All these burdens and pains are on my account.

Searching his armor, I found a piece of parchment, beaten, cracked, and dotted with his blood. As the smoke and death rose from the field of combat, I could not bear to read what might be inscribed upon the parchment. Tucking it inside my armor, I waited for a day when the sun's warmth might find me again, for all was cold in my veins now.

Alexius. A name that in our tongue means companion. Guarder of men. There was no better.

The Myrmidon paused as he let his tears disappear into the cracks of the mortar below his feet.

"And when he came to you, Zeus, I hope he came as a man who resembled the way he had been in life, laughing, and joking, and not the corrupted corpse became in death. I cleaned his body and wrapped him in white linen I removed from my own cot."

"He was hesitant to smile, and to laugh, but eventually he did as he had in life. I saw no corpse, Myrmidon. I saw a man full of happiness and life who only lacked the very essence itself. I was given a glimpse into him."

"And what did you decide of him, Zeus?"

"He was one of the men for whom the flowers bloomed each spring."

Menestheus sent medals and gold to the Myrmidons to aid us in our great victory. He applauded us, though, he had not the time to even visit us in person. We received little more than a scribbled letter and a distant acknowledgment. Still, my friend was dead. These men who occupy the top of the ladder, whether it be in politics, in business, or in the military, are quick to forget the motivations of the lowest soldier; this is to their detriment.

I stacked the wood myself. I laced the pyre with dried reeds and burnt stalks of grass. As I watched him laying atop his resting place my heart blistered like the torch I held in my hand.

Kalliaros, my commander and friend, comforted me as the body burned upon the fire. The anger of the flames reflected upon the gold that sat half-buried in the sand, which we cared nothing for. He put his hand on my back, between the shoulder blades. He spoke as if to his own child.

"Soldiers do not become soldiers because they dream of mighty conquests on foreign shores, praise from their government, or racks of colorful medals denoting their merit pinned across their chest — generals dream of this. The average foot soldier embraces a life of meager pay, probable death, and hard, cold nights where he sleeps scarcely. He talks with joy of home to his brother, wherein he makes sure to include every detail so that he not only settles his own heart, but also gives a piece of his home to the man standing watch on the cold wall beside him.

"When he falls in training or in battle, he will feel in his hands the sand, the blood, and the waning of the sun, but he will not think of Athens, or any sentiment regarding the grandeur of the state or of politics; he will think of home. His eyes will not see the earth he stands upon, but rather the lands of his youth. And if he does die, he will not, in his final moments, see the faces of his generals, or of the king, whose cold and outstretched fingers directed him towards death. Instead, he will see his family, or if he has no family, he might remember a father and son he saw playing beside the river once, in a memory — his personal piece of Elysium. He might see the faces of his friends, as they weep for him. But the soldier dies knowing that his loved ones get to live out the rest of their lives, free from the pain he carried. The soldier, then, dies not for glory, but for peace."

I thanked him for his words. "We must find for ourselves something more than war, or be condemned to stand before funeral pyres for the entirety of our lives."

He nodded in agreement. "Alexius died not for more violence, but for the promise of joy. He understood how limited our time is in this world, and the gift he brought forth was to alleviate the pain from the hearts of warriors. His burden was to change the Myrmidons from bloodthirsty beasts into men. He carried all our humanity in his hands. He need not bear this burden another day."

"I shall carry it for him." I spoke to the fire, and leaned in close, so the heat overwhelmed my eyes. "Save my seat there, friend, next to yours." I took a drink of his illegal wine. It was awful.

Kalliaros patted me on the back. "The gods loved him."

Above, vultures circled. Hanging upon the western wind brought by Zephyrus, the birds always arrived for the feast.

The next day we brought violence to the tall, dark men again. But we knew that our violence was borne from the ambitions of other men, thinly veiled by some quest for glory. We killed, with such hatred, without considering the lives of our enemies. I found this to be the thing that ate away at me most.

Did they not pray to their gods as deeply as we did? Was it a mere competition of piety? While I may have not agreed with nor believed in the same gods as them, the dead men searched for the same salvation we did. Their lives were not devoid of meaning, and in taking the lifeblood from them, we assumed our way of life was the only one worth living. We had, in only the slightest increment, left the path from which we promised to keep.

But I had some hope. Hope for the future and for the day when we could look at our reflections again without reeling. Hope for the day when we could fight for things that pulled our hearts forward instead of acquiescing to the things that pulled our hearts back. I wondered long and hard why we created ambitions that embellished the worst parts of us. I hoped, mostly, for the day, far away, when the auburn sun would set upon the Greek horizon and we could settle knowing that the world was not such a horrific place.

But Egypt we left in smoke and ash. The Argives stayed to enforce Menestheus' rule over the trade industry of the Nile. We sailed the same ocean home, though the ocean was not the same, and neither were we.

I still hope for peace, even in death.

Upon my return from Egypt, I settled into the village life once more. Winter had taken full grip of ur home, and for once, the frost that lined the trees matched that of what I felt inside.

After a long, first sleepless night, I briefed Achilles and the officers about the lessons of war we had learned. As much as I wanted to study the Egyptian tactics, structures, and war morals, I was as interested in the knowledge of our own failures.

But I found myself alone in this pursuit. The other officers, and especially Achilles, wanted to learn of how to enact more violence. They studied only the weaknesses of the enemy. Never again did they sit beside the still lake as instructed. And the mentors knew these men failed but could do nothing to stop them once again. Deimos worked his anger into the trails of the mountain. Iesos fell into a drunken stupor, raving about the power of the gods and their abilities. Teris walked with me and taught me of the different leaves and herbs and their healing qualities. We all searched for what we found most meaningful, but we all ignored what pained us the most.

There was no war immediately following Egypt. We trained our bodies and drilled our tactics, but each night we would return to our homes and our wives and our children, and life was quiet for a while. We had taken up post in a part of Thessaly further to the south than when we had left for Egypt.

Eventually, as they always had, the cinders of conflict sparked again, stoked by greed and power.

We fought the hill tribes of Thrace, whose beards and hair were unkept and wild like their tactics. We conquered the coastal cities of the Hittites. In later years we fought men who, again, we thought were different from ourselves, and this is how we justified their deaths.

But after that, orders came to fight other Greeks, and our justifications shifted once again. The older I became, the more anger I harbored. The anger flared, then turned to quiet desperation, and later, it turned to nothing. My sensations cauterized. Any notion I had of glory or purpose turned to routine. In truth, I knew our souls were dying.

One morning, this life drove me to seek a quiet spot deep in the oldest forest that surrounded our town. The trunks of the trees lay silent, thick with age and in the dying light of the sunset, a brown chestnut color. As the sun set, the edges of their bark glowed orange. They lit the candles of Greece. At dusk they took to their retreat.

In those moments, it was clear to me that the world was not so divided as the men; the forest, at all times, was neither light with hope, nor dark with corruption. At the same time that the trees reached towards the sky with power and hope, they also dug their roots deep into the ground, which gave them stability and understanding. My insignificance as I sat beneath the canopy of the trees, the ancient ones, granted me perspective. And the further I strayed into the natural world, the less the conflict of men overwhelmed my thoughts.

Achilles had been dealing with the politics of war while we had been fighting. When we ran out of enemies, the Myrmidons engaged in further violent inter-warring with the city-states of Greece. The soldiers grew tired and weary. Our rulers exploited our own country. Their passions were weaned on the loveless pursuit of wealth and gain. It was damned pointless. But with further victory, Achilles' bloodlust only grew.

I made myself a home in a small hut beside the river, across from Achilles.

In early spring I saw a woman: Melitta. She was washing linen in the stream, and as she leaned down to ring the white sheets dry, an urge to approach her ripped through my soul. It was something I had never felt before, not in war or training. I wondered if it was peace. I figured peace would be quieter than that.

I asked her to walk the trails with me, and we spoke of the gods and of love. She was the first woman I told the extent of my history to, and this lifted a crushing weight from my shoulders.

She was beautiful, and her black hair sat layered upon her shoulders — a perfect version of my armor, clean, and shining like the midday sun. It harnessed the beauty of the sea when she swam in the Aegean. Most of the time, I would be content with watching her go about life. I found beauty in the smallest of actions: the pouring of hot tea, the slow waking from a deep sleep, and the considerate stares towards the river when she lost herself in thought, hopefully of me.

She asked me once about war, while we walked, hand in hand through the streets. She asked if, in combat, I ever prayed to the gods to stay alive.

"Only in the quiet moments," I said.

Our soldiers did not force themselves upon the town, as we did in combat, but rather we tried to embed our souls into it. We worked the land, built the homes, and visited the market, and we tried once more to become one with the small city. It was my piece of heaven. Still, we were strangers to the people. Some of them accepted us, for their memories stretched longer. We learned much about life from their smiling faces and the way they congregated after supper in the center courtyard. Gardens lined the court, and the citizens tended to them. They met to play games and tell tales to the children.

But we would always be different than them.

I used to wish for war, so they would love me again, if only for a moment.

But with Melitta, no yearning for conflict emerged as it had before. She tore apart everything I thought I knew about life. She loved me, which was more than enough. We drank wine one evening, and as I held the drink and watched her smile at me, I noticed that my hands had stopped shaking and that my heart sat deep and calm beneath my chest.

It may seem trivial to a god, an immortal being… but I assure you, Zeus, since you summoned me to explain what drives all mortal men… Our lives are short and full of uncertainty. When we reflect, we know that it was not the grand gestures that defined us. It was not the conflicts we won, nor the warriors we defeated; it was how we managed the trivial moments, and how we accepted the small things into our hearts. In love, each moment means just as much as the next. Each moment alleviates us, rather than fills us with concern. The trivial moments are the same as they were before love, but the feeling is entirely different. That is what she gave to me.

Achilles and I sat upon the rocks by the sea. They were the same shores we had arrived upon so long ago, and yet, I still felt the same fear, and the compounding dread I held for the safety of my men. Achilles did not carry this weight. He spoke, and he thought only of victory, and war. I pitied him, yet I was jealous of his ability to tune the world out.

Increasingly I had been feeling more uncomfortable, for if the end of war was love then I was certain I had found it. But I was also in debt to my friend and leader and most of all, I was in debt to my men. Between these things my priorities tore like old linen. The beauty of the world had washed away any old ambitions of glory, and yet, I needed to be violent to protect that which I loved.

Achilles summoned me to the beach.

He spoke first.

"I need you to take charge of the trials, for the new boys. Take Deimos, Teris, and Iesos, with you commanding. There are islands in the south, much like ours was. The Myrmidons can liberate them and induct recruits into training. Where they are lost to the sands of time, we will give them purpose."

"I have wanted to be involved in training for quite a while now, I'll admit, but why now, at this moment? Do you wish for your boy to join us?"

"Not yet; he is too young, and too weak of mind for this cycle, but in time he will earn his black armor. It is not the changes in myself, dear friend, but the ones in you that drive me. I've seen how you've transformed. There is no soldier left in you. Your death in war will be unavoidable, should I leave you where you are currently. Your life is much the same as many of ours; most of us have families, and responsibilities. But I need the others. Now is the time to strengthen the Myrmidons with new blood. Yours wanes."

I responded, "You have a family as well as I, Achilles. You should join me. Train a new man for leadership. You've done enough for everyone. Have you not seen enough death for ten lifetimes? Step back. Enjoy your time with your wife and son and leave death behind, until the end of life comes as it does for all men."

"What kind of leader removes himself from all this?"

"The kind whose soul recognizes that a maxim pushed to its edge becomes a sin. Children do not understand death, and if you die in war, all you do is subject them to more loss. Where is his birth father? Deserted. Destitute. You've given them the life you never had, the figure they needed. You would throw that away as well?"

"I throw nothing away," he said, a bit of anger escaping his composure. "I am torn by leadership, and by parenthood. Both are similar, but the consequences are equally devastating. A cold heart I have, Stelios; I lost that which is human long ago — I cannot take with me into battle such weakness… What would you have me do?"

"Transition the experience to another to lead, and use the men you have so you may live your life. Those who did not choose the life of family can carry the Myrmidons. Pick a new leader of the army so that they might execute the code we've created."

Achilles was silent for a while. In his heart he knew the right thing to do, but men seldom look towards their truthful hearts, for they fear the answer.

I broke the silence. "Can you not detach from it? In another life we are old men sitting by the sea, watching the wild horses trample the morning dew from the fields. They are free. We might be one day as well.

"In my heart I wish I were so lucky as to have inherited your relentlessness for war. But alas, I cannot close my eyes to that which I have witnessed… But can you not see beyond all this, Achilles?"

He thought for a moment. "No. Where you see peace, I see conflict. In my heart there is only an ocean of fire. There are no horses, only chariots of war. The drops that run in beads down the blades are crimson, not clear. Do not envy me, Stelios. It is not a virtue now, but a vice. It wakes me from deep slumber. Since Rhodes, I see war in every grain of sand and in every piece of peeling bark on the trees. And when I return home, it is no different. Tactics are forged and battle strategies considered at the dinner table. Methods of death are conjured in the quiet of the river, even when I sit peacefully with my love. Do not make the mistake of ever holding jealously about my talent. It eats away at my bowels like an insect. It never vacates…"

He paused and bowed his head.

"I fear I can never leave."

He stared at the ocean. I prayed he was mistaken. "Is saving them, your wife and son, not enough for you? How can it not be enough?"

Nothing will ever be enough, Stelios. Go see the quartermaster. I've seen to it that he has enough gear for you, and he is waiting. Do not keep him long. Take the boats in the morning and the men, spend your last night for a while here at home, kiss your wife, and sleep well tonight. I shall do the same, and I will consider what you've said. I shall give you leave each month to sail back and visit your family…" he trailed off.

I put my hand on his shoulder, but he reeled at the sentiment. "I shall retire to my home for the evening, Achilles. In my prayers I shall consider the consequences of a life lived only for war."

"Goodnight," he answered.

I gave no explanation to Melitta—she needed none. I had told her all about the way we shaped young men, and the method that had shaped me.

She spoke to me that evening, as we laid bare atop the bed and felt the cool breeze across our skin.

"You are the best choice, because your intentions are uncorrupted."

"But do I not merely sentence these boys to a life I myself no longer love?"

She considered this. "Though it may no longer define you, it still serves as the foundation you built yourself upon. There are boys like you who need saving from the cruelty of men — perhaps one day the Myrmidons will see the truth. For now, focus on the next step you must take, my love."

On the morning we left, the sky burned red. The sun cracked the gentle horizon. I packed my gear, and I kissed her as Achilles had asked. She sat on the shore as our white sails billowed in the wind.

I could consider the pain and suffering of the future, but at that moment I had a task, and in the concentration of tasks I forgot my hardships, if only for a moment.

We set sail to free children condemned to the same fate, the same youth that we had been subject to — a brutal task, but finally, a worthy one.

VII

TARTARUS IS EMPTY

The ocean gave us pleasant weather and fortune. The sea and her anger, when provoked, could be a far superior enemy to any we could face, and so we rejoiced in her mercy. The brutality of the churning waves, when pressed, can sink an army in an evening. As powerful and as disciplined as we were, our courage fell short in the face of the immensity of nature, and of the gods that controlled it.

Kalliaros and his platoon of twenty men came for the voyage, as did Teris. Kalliaros, as he had always done, volunteered his time and peace to accompany me on the journey. To be completely truthful, his experience and grasp on life exceeded my own, so I felt deep within my heart that I needed his guidance.

Night fell. Kalliaros approached me on the bow of the ship as I watched the white tips of the waves crackle and separate then settle among the green phosphorus of the ocean. We soldiers had little to do at sea other than speak to one another.

"It makes you feel small," he said to me, "and yet purposeful. Our existence is a part of something much larger than ourselves. Yet again, this truth presents itself to me, here in the arena of the elements. I acknowledge this, and so I am free."

"To attach one's soul to a fate which one has no control over is healthy in the journey of living," I responded, still spellbound by the black waves of the night.

He laughed, "Ah! My friend, a philosopher! Do not think too deeply young soldier, for thoughts will swallow you whole."

His laugh pained me. Every laugh after Alexius died was painful.

"It is my nature. They come to me in the dark of the night and torture my sleep. They approach me unsolicited in the streets, and in the moments when the eyes of my wife slowly close, drawing down with the dusk as I speak lullabies to her. They swim like eels towards me as I swim with the children in the river. I can't help such things…"

I looked at him.

"What must I do?"

"As with all things, you must endure. You must open your heart to life's crests and troughs — the oceans of our happiness and our sadness are not separate but rather churned and mixed in the whirlpool of meeting tides. Our thoughts force us to deal with the hardships and the triumphs forced upon us, despite our preparation to do so, and to undergo similar confrontations with the same fervor, no matter how devastating those oscillations are."

"And we must accept the storm regardless of what time of the day it reaches us," I said.

"Or the night," he added. Kalliaros continued.

"The highest endeavor is to endure the most extreme and the most inconsequential hardships of life with the same fervor, so that whatever might occur settles in an equivalent way — in a way that does not compromise character. The role of the gods, I believe, in their supernatural power over the earth, is to facilitate these tests unto us."

"For what purpose? Which god records these findings? Would it not be better to bring us constant joy and happiness?" I asked.

"No such thing exists, my young friend."

In the distance we could now see the ghostly outline of the island.

"Our role is to observe your reactions to such trials. To let them unfold. Not to bend the tree until it snaps," Zeus interjected.

We rowed as the wind died down and the sails of our ship hung like gentle sheets of morning linen after a calm night. We rowed not with the haste of impending battle, but with the resistance of thought. Most of our men had been children of a similar island, and so they knew the implications of our mission. This may have been a different island in a different time, and the world may have changed since our youth. The crimes of man, however, had changed little. We knew little of this new place, the children who lived there, or the men who housed them for labor, and yet we knew it all intimately. As we approached the island, I felt the horrors of my youth creeping up my spine.

I feared what these horrors might do to me, but as men, these horrors presented themselves to us each time we removed our armor.

Though a sword's slash left revered gouges upon our armor, the whip lashes of our youth left raised pink scars, found underneath. I had seen my men immediately following battle. I had seen the victory in their eyes, the welling up of self-belief in their hearts and in each other. But I knew the cruelty of their origin, and I wondered how such broken children could become such heroic men.

I remember the cold nights on the farm, where we slept in the barn in the middle of the walkway while the animals made their beds against the walls. We wanted for nothing, nor did we think in very profound terms, for we had no hope, and we had no notions of the world.

We saw death there too.

"Although we did not live, we were still scared to die. Deep within that feeling, I found a belief in the gods, and you, Zeus. And when I realized that the degradations of men could not touch our internal fires, I found optimism."

"Are soldiers scared to die? I cannot comprehend the feeling for myself."

"We were not afraid to die. We were afraid of what we might miss.

"And we were not scared as youth, but I remember our bodies — the skeletons we carried around. I feel it now, the weakness in our arms and legs and the burning headaches from the lack of food that resulted in the slow dying and decay of our bodies and our adolescence. We were dead in a way already. We prayed but received nothing in response.

"It is then the cruelest state of living — to burn with belief but to feel only depression and distress. It challenges the human heart to the frontiers of conviction and faith."

"The horrors of man are not the work of the gods. We create in the hope we create beauty. The warrior. The politician. The mother. All of these are crafted, but their creators become hostages. We watch the choices made by the things we create. We are bound like prisoners. And, if the choices of our conceptions cause suffering, we carry this in our hearts forever."

The shores of the island came closer. The gods kept clouds lingering above them. The sky, once blue and clear, was now dark and full of shadows.

I had no recollection of when this change occurred. My thoughts had taken me far away.

In adulthood we had experienced redemption in Greece, totalitarianism in Rhodes, and divine ambition in Egypt, but those men on that island remain the lowest forms of humans we ever encountered.

The streets sat quiet and dim. Homes crumbled, and the stones, which lay in ruins, had piled upon them a black ash which rained from the clouded sky. We entered. The smoke rose in wisps from the ground. The underworld presented itself to us. Men scattered like rats amid the mazed streets. In a diamond formation we moved and navigated. Crouched and with weapons drawn we crept further into the town. The air stood still. With each step, my chest grew tighter — it was like breathing underwater.

We rounded the corner — a crack like a breaking tree tore through the night. A lithe figure slammed into the Myrmidon next to me. I immediately stuck the ghostly figure and shoved him to the ground. The attacker fell, blood draining from his flank. The moonlight reflected from his shaved head, and his hollow cheeks gave him a skull-like quality that defined his face.

The Myrmidon next to me was Teris. He had been stuck with the knife, but the wound was shallow, and he would survive. Teris reached between the plates of his armor and ripped the protruding weapon from his flesh. I took a handful of clay and pressed it hard into his midsection to stem the bleeding. Teris grimaced as the pain elevated, but he was as tough as hell itself. He let out an angry exhale and raked his boot across the attacker's gaunt face. He lifted the blood-smeared knife towards me, and I examined the small weapon.

No. It was not a knife.

It was a small bone, sharpened to a deadly edge. The very fibers of my soul frayed as I held it in my grasp.

Though the enemy consisted of an unorganized force, they still killed some of our men. Their scattered attacks and tactics made it so that we did not fight a war, but rather a shadow. They were not a single line of soldiers, steady across the field, staring, clad in emboldened armor, and bound to a code of war. We fought physical manifestations of desperation. We fought pure evil.

As the forest appeared from behind the smoke, three of the gaunt men appeared and threw spears from the haze. They rang true upon our raised shields, but it shocked me to feel the force behind them. Our enemy may have been a shadow, but they knew war as well. We held our lines. The attacks continued and came from all sides at all times.

Emerging from the burning town into a field of smoke and huts, we saw the faces of the children. No nightmare contends nor death compares to the feeling of seeing those gaunt and emaciated expressions. We spoke to them. They said nothing back. The children were so ingrained in their torture and subjugated for so long a time, even we could not convince them of their liberty. Freedom meant nothing to them, and we were just more armed men — another group of violent souls.

We kept walking, collecting children on the way, and sending them to the rear ranks. We turned many over whose faces we found buried in the dirt. Through the smoke, stray dogs shuffled and growled as we reached the camps beyond the town.

I prayed to the gods I would never find out what kept the dogs fed.

The sites we encountered were destitute. Beaten, worked to the bone, and robbed of their youth and spirit, the children looked mournfully into our eyes. My body shook with something far deeper than anger; an ineffable rage took over.

The enemy had scattered into the woods. Their footsteps echoed through the smoke from the trees. We killed their countrymen on our way through the city, but I would do far worse if I ever got a hold of them.

The children stumbled like ghosts towards us. Still carrying their tools and bags, they shuffled like a slow tide. We gently removed the weights from their arms, but they tried to take them back, blindly moving towards their next task. They did not truly look at us, not like young people should. It was the absence of happiness, or even of fear, which struck our hearts, for the youth had no regard for us or for themselves.

Warriors around me broke down with the sight of it all.

It was the fires, the piles of garbage, and the bodies. It was the image of the children back home that they saw in their eyes.

We moved further into the darkness, and though we remained on high alert, our senses blurred.

That is when we found their homes, though I hate to use such a word. The children had crudely constructed shelters. Made of mud and clay, with no true roof or walls, the structures lay barren and desolate. The bones of the home were so thin and unstable that they resembled the bodies of the children who inhabited them.

Even as I hear my recounting of this island, I know I fail to convey the severity of it. Some calamities in life are so severe that sight is the only sense that remembers. We were soldiers no more, not when we saw the children, sitting in the cold mud, whose hair had turned ashen with the falling debris.

I realized then that the dark clouds in the sky rained the remains of the dead boys and girls, and the dense air we had been breathing which now lined our lungs was the ash of burnt bodies.

I gagged and coughed and tried to control my horror, but I vomited and dropped to one knee amidst the terror.

In those moments, we Myrmidons were not heroic. It was as if in the face of true evil, we had reverted to mere men, to fathers and husbands, and to the broken children we once were on the inside.

In our cruel twist of fate and fortune, we were the only men that could comprehend their pain. There we stood, the most disciplined men of Greece, the ones who did not give out their black armor nor yield to any enemy, great or small, and the sight of young children had broken us completely.

The very image had broken my mind with the force of a shattering shield, and I lost my focus in the moment when I needed it most.

In our shock and disgust, our men cracked and shattered, and it was in that moment that the ghosts attacked us again, in greater force and with the element of shock. They came at us like apparitions of the island, emboldened by their final act. To the right was a line of forest where low mist hung at chest height; behind us, screams filled the air; and to the immediate front we faced the charge of desperate men. We had lost battle awareness, and now we were surrounded. Our minds needed to adjust back to warriors'.

Their desperation gave them an edge, in that they wanted not to die a soldier's death, of honor, but rather that they wanted to slash and cut and injure us as much as possible. It did not matter to them how cowardly their acts were, only that they made others suffer in every way.

No generals commanded them. Their insanity cried battle commands. Their advantage was their tactical position, but we cut them down with a rage for what they had done.

In that bloodlust and chaos, the fog of war rolled across the field. No longer could I see the trees. Men flew at us as if from dust, lurking in the shadows and striking without warning. We sliced them into pieces, but did not emerge unscathed.

Bone knives protruded from our powerful thighs. Blood poured from gashes on the exposed upper shoulders of the Myrmidons. The fog began to lift in the trees as we murdered them. Yes, we murdered them. It was not war. I gave them no honors nor mercy. I did not afford them a single scrap of pity as I would have done to an enemy in a uniform.

And that's when we saw it. Bodies. Stacked row upon row. A wall. Sitting within the trees, and constructed for no purpose, it was so nefarious and cruel that our minds could not comprehend it. They were just children. Tiny hands and fingers lay limp and hung in the air. And, at the height of this horror, my mentor and friend, Kalliaros, stood to look at me in horror at the sight of the atrocity.

I tried to find the words to comfort him, "Look away, my friend, stay calm. Focus on the battle — "

An earsplitting rupture of bone and flesh interrupted my speech. The sharp point of a spear exploded from his abdomen. Amid the smoke and fog, I saw the recognition of death in his eyes.

The man who drove it through his stomach had approached us as a stalker from the trees. We were the soldiers of the night but all we could see was the fog. Kalliaros had not seen the man sneaking through the trees, none of us had. And while my friend's eyes had filled with tears and his mind raged at the sight of the evil in front of him, he did not hear the crackling branches that broke under the feet of the attacker.

We hacked the enemy to death. I could not stop. I lost control and my blade went through skin, through bone and brain, and I kept hacking the dirt when there was nothing left. Kalliaros dropped to his knees and helplessly clutched the point of the steel as it protruded from his organs. He was a soldier to the bitter end. His trembling arms grappled with the sharp metal. He ripped the pine spear from his body with aggression. He did so not because he thought it would save his life, in fact, he knew he would die, but because it was the noblest thing he could do in his last moment. It was murder, plain and simple. The worst part, the one that destroyed me, as the cold breath of the ferryman raised the hairs on Kalliaros' neck, was that despite the warrior's brilliant and noble life, the final thing he saw was the absolute lowest degree of mankind — the vilest possible demonstration of pain enacted by the evilest souls of men.

This man was privy to only that vision upon death, having lived so heroically.

My heart would have broken knowing this fact if it had not been shattered a thousand times already.

Each piece of my shattered heart I left scattered throughout the world, buried in the ground with each one of my friends who died.

Someone grabbed my arm and stopped me. My sword had fractured. Shards of metal lay scattered throughout the battleground. Without realizing, I had shattered the blade to fragments as I'd repeatedly slammed it into the hard stones underneath the enemy.

Blood spray and pieces of the man covered my entire body.

My anger had consumed me. I did not recognize who that Stelios was. He was a monster, just like they had said… While ripping the man to pieces I'd felt nothing. The lack of any sensation scared me more than the fury itself.

I carried the body of Kalliaros, commander, second battalion of the

Myrmidons, fifty feet to the rear and covered his now mangled corpse in one of the blankets we had brought for the children.

I dropped his body briefly to finish the mission. I would not leave him here. I would have carried him upon my shoulders, through the depths of the Aegean, if necessary, to bring him home. But one of the cruelest parts of war is that you cannot stop when your friends die.

I turned back to press on. Wrought with devastating sadness I willed my feet forward, but I could not figure out which way to go. It was as if my intestines had been ripped out and used for fishing line. In that moment, my mind slipped, and my concentration blurred, but from the smoke, a boy approached me. His eyes spoke for his heartache and his stare took grip of my heart. Though I wanted nothing more than to cry and sob, I saw the remaining color in his eyes, and I used his hope to stand tall. As he neared me, I removed my spaulders, the armor that covered my shoulders. Kneeling before him I tried to cast a less threatening figure. I spoke to him in an attempt to let him know that he would now be safe.

He had short, scruffy brown hair, and his skin wrinkled like he had spent too long in the sea.

He looked at me, and in his figure, I saw the image of youth. That piece of me, the innocence I knew from the river, suffered knowing he was someone's son, and that fate had abandoned him in such a way.

It filled me with contempt, hate, and a longing for justice and for the world to stop being such a horrid place, if only for a moment. But the world does not give us such reprieves. So instead of waiting for a gift, I took the moment for myself, and placed my shoulder guards on the boy's body. My armor, the part of me that made me into a man, melded into a part of him, and I rapped the bottom of my closed fist against the hard metal that now sat upon his small chest.

I spoke to him. I spoke to him in the same manner the soldier on the boat, back when we left the farm, had spoken to me. I remembered the soldier who saved me so long ago and the way he had dragged me from hell with his words alone. In times of strife, soldiers always fall back on their training, which is why it is taken so seriously.

"What you are is not what you might become. What you are now is not as important as what you might be. It is not your fault, but it is now your choice. Take this armor and use it as your shield against the world. Find a pond, a still pond, where the world is simple, and gaze at your reflection with my armor on your shoulders. The end of this life is now. The slate is clean. Put your heart into your self-belief and find strength in your suffering.

"Only simple footsteps bring us through hell; we cannot attempt to leap across it." I spoke to him as I walked him to the ship, right arm wrapped tightly around the blanket that sat across his small shoulders.

"Be nothing now but the master of your own fate in this moment, and be courageous enough to stride from the things which hurt you the most, but which also define you here on this ground — challenge the first obstacle, my son. Turn the mountain into a ladder."

I found no further words for my throat closed with threat of weeping, my voice cracking in my attempt.

The boys had no obligation to become soldiers, nor to even come with us, but we promised them freedom and at the very least, a voyage away from their place of pain. Once in Thessaly, we would need to help them recover before allowing them to challenge the training, or to send them on their way.

We loaded the living ones into the boats. The dead ones we buried. We could not stand to burn them, even though this is our tradition. We could stand no more fire, nor smoke. As we sailed through the haze, the ones who we could save cast their parting gaze upon their island with little remorse.

"Rest now. The Myrmidons have the watch. No harm will befall you here," we said to them, as softly as we could.

On the long voyage we spoke to them, asked them their names, what they remembered of their lives, and recounted stories of the Myrmidons and of Achilles.

But mostly they slept.

They were weary. I had to check that some of them were still alive. In sleep they looked at peace, and so we left them to rest beneath the soft blankets while we rowed the boats to Thessaly.

Despite this, the gods still took some of them from us. I shall never understand why.

Three of the children were too far gone and suffered from extreme hunger and thirst. No matter how much we fed them, or how much water we gently poured down their throats, their already tiny bodies continued to shrink and wither.

I watched the Myrmidons put pieces of dried bread into their mouths.

I watched as rough men's faces held firm as they helped them. Their focused and determined eyes wrought with sadness, they breathed through their noses, for they could not speak. I watched as the stream of tears ran from their cheeks and dripped, slowly, from the bottoms of their beards.

But we almost saved them all. We wrapped their shrunken bodies in linen and, as gently as possible, the strong arms of Leandros and Teris gifted them to the god we knew would cradle them and hold their small heads in its arms — the sea.

No man complained. I told Teris to take refuge in my quarters below, urging his body to rest. His wound bubbled with blood. He responded with reddened and sad eyes, "No, let me watch over them. I shall not sleep upon a feathered mattress this night. I shall gain my rest from knowing they have theirs, if you allow it."

"Who am I to refuse such things," I replied.

The men were anxious. I was filled with heartache.

I needed to seek refuge in the words of my colleagues, or risk falling into the abyss of my mind. "Leandros," I summoned. The lion-man had his giant forearms wrapped around a tiny girl with soft brown hair. Below deck, he had helped her wash the residue from her locks, and after that she'd fallen into a deep sleep as he'd cradled her.

"Speak with me, my friend. How could men allow such horrors to manifest?" I asked.

He stood and sighed. The bags which hung from his eyes suggested to me that the man had rested little if at all, much like the others, but he was so valiant by nature, so stoic, and he assumed so much of what the origin of his name suggested that he still looked primed for battle. "Whoever these men were, they lost themselves long ago," he began, "but men are not born this way. They corrupt, and then the system does not redeem their hearts. It rewards exploitation and power. We Myrmidons combat that which is evil, yet we are mere extensions of power. I feel despair in my heart, sir. I know not how to continue after this. My armor may soon sit upon the shining hill, and I shall find a hole to crawl into and die, for it would be simpler at this point than understanding where the world has gone."

"And if you do such a thing, what happens to the others? Do not be so naïve, my friend, there are others. What then? Though it is painful beyond measure, we might find that the impossibility of our countless decisions actually ending up somewhere decent and brave is so improbable that when it occurs, we question it with the entirety of our being. We must make the right call, at all times."

He looked at me with a desperation I had never seen in him before. "What difference can one soldier make?" he asked.

"We know we have a burden that we must carry, but one that may define us for the rest of time. Never once did we say that the path would be easy, my friend. Look at this boy here." I pointed to the child I had met and carried to the ship. His soft eyelids reflected the rays of the sun. The light nestled upon them, but they stayed closed. He'd made a meager bed on the deck of the ship; it was more than anything he'd ever had.

The weight of the world was lifted from his shoulders by us.

"I want him to grow and gain strength, and to learn the way of the warrior so that his life can be altered in such a direction that allows him to properly live. Do you not want the same?"

"Of course I do."

"Then don the armor of your heart, lion-man. Children need parents to follow, and if they do not have them, as we didn't, then they need warriors — the kind who carry swords as well as the kind who do not."

He shut his eyes, took a long, slow breath, and finally nodded, but I could still see the uncertainty in him. He took his place on the oak boards next to the girl again.

I looked at the boy. In that moment, I wanted nothing more in the world than to give him a warm bed under a steady roof, to kiss him on the forehead and tell him that everything would be alright now, and most importantly, for him to believe it. I could adopt the boy into our family. I had no way of communicating this with Melitta, but I knew my wife, and I knew she would not hesitate. We wanted children. We had been praying for one ever since we met. And I felt some unmistakable connection to the boy. The rocking of the ocean drew me nearer to him.

It was not a connection born of blood, or guilt, or of pity. It was rather one of those rare moments a man might experience once or twice in his life. It was the one of those flashes that connects the lives of the broken, where it appeared that every defining moment we'd endured, and every piece of chaos led us down countless paths to this one. We made endless decisions, where we faltered and where we found ourselves lost, where the gods converged, and steered our spirit in the right direction, but did not give us the map, and where we found ourselves colliding with purpose.

Although it seemed simple, this particular decision meant more to me than winning endless battles in black armor — it was a legacy worth enduring for.

VIII

THE GODS WE OVERLOOKED

Our journey home felt far longer than the one we took to leave it. Our arrival forced us to rouse the sleeping children, whose faces awoke with just a bit more color and happiness than when they'd fallen asleep. For that, we gave thanks, but we hated waking them all the same. Achilles had given me orders to bring the youth straight to the training island, and for a moment as he made his way towards the dock, his face contorted with anger at the breaking of his instructions.

"Stelios! What are you…?" he began, but could not finish his sentence.

We helped the children off of the high boats, and their feet fell upon the warm beach. Achilles stopped. His lean figure churned up the ground beneath him.

I had no will to fight with him today, and none of us had slept since we'd left. He looked at the young ones as they wondered at the beauty of their new home and shuffled in file across the beach. But the shadow of Achilles cast a dark blanket over them. He stared at them, calculating, and judging each one by how useful they might be. I said nothing but bowed my head in fatigue and continued to lift the tiny bodies from the boat.

Each pair of small hands that clasped mine solidified my choice.

Though Achilles only understood war, this was something else entirely. Selfishly, I hoped that the sight of them might trigger something within him. Secretly, I hoped that they might be able to do the thing that I'd never accomplished: save the soul of Achilles.

Purple gardens lined the stone courtyard next to the shore. Evening was falling, and the sun was glowing on the ocean. Achilles said nothing to us, but instead he walked across the soft sand, put his hand on my shoulder to reassure me, even though he knew it would not help, and began helping us unload the children. He sent word to the village that each family need make extra beds and hot food.

My strength to endure was failing. I needed to find her.

I spoke to my general. "Achilles, this boy here," I nodded to my new son, "I will take into my household, but I must speak to Melitta first. Might you comfort him, only for a few moments?"

Achilles nodded but his eyebrows rose with the inconvenience. He picked the boy up into his arms, his hands lacking a gentle touch. Nothing within him resembled softness. I spoke to the child.

"I will be right back, son. This man will protect you."

The boy trusted me, and so he trusted my blonde-haired friend.

I took off up the path, searching for her. Word would have spread now concerning our arrival. She would be coming to meet me, but every step, every effort I made to move, resulted in more anxiety and pain. I wanted nothing more than to scream. Chrysanthe passed me along the trail, looking for her husband, and, as she always did, walked elegant and regally.

"Stelios," she said, "what's wrong?"

"Where is she?" was all that I could muster.

"Minutes behind. Keep going and you shall find her," she said. "Wait." She grabbed me by the armor and shifted it back to center. She wiped the dirt from my cheek and clipped my hair back behind my ear.

She did not say out loud, "Steel your courage, soldier. Your wife awaits you," but her actions implied it, and I nodded in thanks. Chrysanthe accepted in her presence only the sturdiest man. My wife was different, but I appreciated that piece of tough love.

I found Melitta as I approached the town center, where the pink and white campanula flowers hung from the baskets that lined the road. Chrysanthe had given me strength with her nature, but when I saw Melitta's chestnut eyes among the beauty, every ounce of pain that I had kept locked away within me shattered. I shook and fell to the ground, grabbing at her sleeves.

She said nothing, for she had never seen me in such a state. On the smooth stones of the courtyard and under the now darkening sky of Greece, she held my head in comfort. When I was able to speak, I recounted the horrors of the past voyage. I left details out.

"This boy you speak of, we must help him. We must take him in," she implored, without my asking.

"Without you, my world would cease, my love," I replied to her. "How would I continue without you, after shouldering these things which haunt me?"

"You shall never need to know a world without me, Stelios. Let me go and meet him." She was such a loving and gentle soul, I was sure the boy would latch onto her immediately, as I had.

"He is with Achilles," I replied.

"Ah, then let us fetch him before Achilles has him sparring at the arena, training for glorious combat." And I laughed, to the extent I could, and wiped the tears from my eyes. She did her best to stop my suffering, though she was just as broken as I from the tale.

That night I slept on the cold floor, for I could not bring myself to accept the comforts afforded to me. That night I dove into my youth. I dreamed the horrors of my memory, and in the countless bouts of awakening that night I realized that only in my dreams could I revisit a place of such intense agony — only my dreams could recreate such atrocities.

The floor I slept on, while hard and icy, did not hold the same imperceptible and crushing hardness that the ground of my childhood did. I decided to walk because the frigid air set an iron weight upon my chest.

I checked once more on Melitta, whose chest rose and fell like the tide. Her soft arm was wrapped around the boy's midsection. He slept comfortably, and soundlessly. It was only my soul that was still tortured, and I would carry that as I had promised.

I set upon the quiet streets of the town. Beside the metalworker's shop, a group of elderly men sat and discussed their lives and laments, as they did each night. I sat, apart from them, but in earshot, so that I could find out for myself what old men, who had not died young and beautifully in battle, regretted in their old age. There were three of these old friends, grizzled and tired, and though to my eye their joints and tendons ached with the weight of life, they sat with straight backs and broad shoulders, even though it caused them discomfort. As I went to leave, they saw me appear from the darkness and the implored me to join them.

"Sit down, young soldier," the first man spoke amicably, and with the soft touch of a grandfather. "What torments you so?"

"Is it obvious?" I chuckled, feeling at ease in their presence.

"Old men search for answers in the peace of the night. Old men do this, or young men who have seen far too much for their age."

"Did you see them?" I asked, speaking of the children.

They nodded. "We did," said one, " and we have seen things like this before. It is much more shattering to a young man… time will heal them, and it will heal you too, warrior. But the world forgets its evils, and so is bound to repeat them."

The seniors discussed the painful things in their life, but all of them held immense pride for the heavy things they'd endured.

"My son is a blacksmith, who travels the trade route down the coast," another one said. "His heart is happy and light."

Another spoke, "My wife passed last year. And so now I am stuck with these old, wrinkled friends." He laughed, pained. "But they are friends nonetheless."

All of them had faced the things that scared them the most in the world. They did not dismiss the gods as vicious, though they had suffered at their hands.

"Soldier," the first one addressed me.

"Sir?" I replied.

"You see, even though your spirit burns, you still retain your dignity. I am no officer, nor leader, and yet you still address me as such."

"Habit," I laughed. And the man chuckled, but his eyes remained locked to mine.

"My children are farmers. They wake with the dawn. They work harder than anyone I know. Trust me, a day on the farm would have even the mighty Achilles rubbing his back at the finish. In the evenings, they have bread and soup made from fresh tomatoes and thyme. Can you smell it, young warrior? Can you see the steam from the bowl rise and fly from the open window into the cool night?"

I nodded. I could. I could see each piece of the untroubled home. I heard the family tell jokes to one another. I saw the father playfully chase the son around the table while the mother jokingly scolded the boys for acting like animals in the middle of dinner, but she laughed all the same.

"I can. Every piece of it."

"And at night, such as the one we live now, what do you hear? What noises are present in your mind, as my children and grandchildren slumber?"

I closed my eyes. "Wind, howling through the trees. Animals from the shelter, sleeping, but shuffling and moving in their rest. The chirping of insects, rhythmic and soothing."

He put his hand on my shoulder. "Peace," he stated. "Lightness of the heart earned and protected by warriors who walk the streets at night and grapple with the demons inside them. Peace, while the men with black armor repel those who would try to take such things from them." He paused.

"I pray to the gods that for all your sacrifice, you find such peace someday."

I sat there most of the night, even after the men had gone to bed. Dawn approached, and brought with it that renewal that, as boys, enveloped us with fear, but as men we craved. Removing the parchment from my armor, which was still dotted with the blood of my friend, I carefully unfolded the tattered paper. I remembered Alexius, and how he could make even the most elderly men laugh as if they were teenagers again. I thought of his smiling face, and how Alexius was able to be the torch in the night of this world. I missed him. The paper had inscribed upon it these words:

IN DISTANT PAST, WHEN FATE SEEMED SET,
INSIDE A WRETCHED PIT,
A FACELESS FATHER LEFT ME THERE,
MY CHANCE AT LIFE FORFEIT,
BUT BROTHERS PULLED ME FROM THAT DARK
THESE MEN I LOVE AND HOLD,
STRANGER, POINT THESE MEN WHERE I SLUMBER,
DO NOT BURY ME WITH GOLD,
IF GODS AND TIME DEEM DIE WITH FRIENDS,
THEN DRAW ME FROM MY SHADE,
FOR I'LL NOT FIND SUCH LOYAL KIN,
WHO HELD THE THINGS THEY WEIGHED,
IF I BURN NOW AMONG THE ASH,
IF EMBERS FLICKER BY THE COAL
CRY NOT, FOR ON THE HEARTS OF ANTS
INVINCIBLE MY SOUL.

Red, burning torches lined the streets. I placed the poem in the middle of the fire and watched the remains drift into the starry sky.

And when I returned, the boy was still fast asleep.

Life is suffering, but dreams grant us insight to the pain and bring truth to the reality.

Dreams allow us to reach untested heights, to pit our mettle against the dark creative corners of the psyche, to face the monsters, the three-headed snakes, with fangs like knives that penetrated flesh and bone, and to encounter the war-god Ares, whose prophecies about our lives filled us with purpose. Life, however, is the slow ticking of the clock that ages the earth, while we lay awake in the cold endless abyss.

The abyss that I remember was so inflexible and unflinching and immovable that it wore away the gritty fragments of sanity, like a crashing sea against stone, and in the light of the moon that evening it dragged me, wanting and unwitting, through the painful slow night.

I prayed his dreams were light and peaceful, as mine had never been.

The boy slept in my place, and in moments when he awoke, I saw the glint of his eyes in the moonlight. Though I wanted desperately to speak with him, I too had a sense for timing; that night would grant us no movement forward. The silence and the absence of peril had to be enough to satisfy us until the dawn.

The distant but approaching dawn.

In the morning I awoke having slept little, and I showed the boy around the house. He seemed pleased about the small items, and the normality of it all. He was still quiet, but happy, and we took a slow walk along the river as I had some time before I was to meet Achilles to debrief him.

"What is your name, son?"

"I do not remember."

"When were you born?"

"I know not. I remember only the work, and the island."

"The same is true for all the boys?"

"Yes."

"Then you will all need to remember. In our names we carry our legacies. Our names live on as we define ourselves through our actions.."

I looked at him, studying his features. "Think hard on your past. Do not discard it completely, for it shall shape you in some way. But take the day, or days, and find some scrap of hope buried deep within the horrors of your upbringing. Come to terms with faith for the future."

I pulled the piece of old sail out from the inside of my linen. "This is mine."

He looked up at me. "I understand."

Zeus spoke, *"Men find the gods only when they withdraw their fixed gaze from the pinnacle of the mountain and focus on the grains of sand which compose it."*

The Myrmidon looked at the pillars of the temple. "But our mortal eyes are attracted to the peaks of the snow-capped mountains. I fear this is Hades calling to us once again, dragging us away from the importance of the small beauties in our lives. Can we not be happy? Why do we always yearn for more?"

Later that day I met Achilles near the boats and explained my decision. I recounted the terror of the scene, the state of the men who had been with me. I told him that they had not slept on the journey home. I asked about the health of the children, and I was adamant that we could not take them to training right away.

"Now is the time," he argued. "Breaking them will only make them stronger warriors."

"Not if you break them completely. I know your passion for war, my friend, but have our lives not been unquestionably changed? Have we not seen the other side? How can we possibly go back after this? We must think differently now."

"My passion for war remains, old friend, but I fear yours has fallen too far."

"And if it has, you will question my ability, my allegiance? I, who have lost so greatly?"

He ignored my prod. "You have a week for them to rest, but your sails will be raised by the harvest moon."

His shining blonde hair twisted as he turned to leave, but I lost my temper with him.

"And what treachery do we commit by inducting them to this life with such haste!? Where shall you stop, great Achilles? Shall it be the borders of the known earth that swallow you whole, or just your own desires? What life is this to lead until the breath of time expires and exhales its judgement unto us? Just soldiers, we are then, and nothing more."

"Tell me, Stelios," he snarled back, "do our men still fall in battle? Are they still susceptible to steel and arrow?"

"Of course, they are but mortals."

"Then my goal has not been met. For though we pursue, we are not perfect. I shall stand for no less in this regiment. I shall not sleep until we conquer all those who, in the peace of their distant homes, think themselves better than our ranks."

"You would wage war on the entire world then, Achilles, for these men you speak of do not exist. They manifest only in your thoughts. Their armor is mineral, built and woven by your beliefs, and their swords are diamond, forged by your hate and resentment. It will kill us all."

"Then die glorious deaths we shall. I will accept no less, and even in death I shall whip these men in the underworld for their weakness."

I shook my head at his stubbornness. I still believed he was a good man, but our ideals had split from each other.

I would need a week at least, and then a slow start to training as not to break the children. They would need food, and rest, and time spent in the outdoors with no agenda, schedule, or men telling them exactly what to do. We'd allow them to be kids for a moment, then help them become adults.

Unfortunately, we could not give them back what they had lost to time. We could not replace their youth. But it wouldn't be healthy to delay the maturity of these adolescents on the precipice of adulthood, as that would not help them either. It was just the cruel falling of fate, unavoidable, sometimes. All we can do is accept it, and try to mold ourselves into someone who can withstand it.

The storm comes for us all.

At the end of that week, the children looked far healthier and far stronger. I thought how incredible it was that the smallest piece of freedom, happiness, and guidance could transform the spirit. I can honestly say I did extraordinarily little other than answer questions when asked, and demonstrate proper technique when it flagged. When curiosity flourished, I answered what I could.

During this time of delight, I prepared my armor and readings for the journey. My boy had not remembered his name yet. He spent many hours diving deep into his memories, and though it pained him, it made him stronger.

Our last evening together was bliss. Melitta and I laughed, in good spirits. The red sky burned across the sea and the village, making its landing in the river next to our home. We drank red wine that she had fermented the month before from the hills of Thessaly. The grapes she used ripened in a longer period than those of Attica, to the south, where wine was the primary drink of the regiment. As the wine touched my lips, I spoke to her, "This wine reminds me of you."

She laughed. "Sour, and dry?"

"Patient, and with that patience a less acidic taste for life."

Her eyes were soft and understanding.

"Are all warriors such students of poetry?"

"Most warriors avoid such things. Otherwise, they think too deeply on what they've done."

Our boy sat by the river, fifteen feet away, skipping rocks across its moving shelf of water. He rejoiced each time he made more than three hops. He celebrated like a child should, for what was certainly for the first time in his brutal life, and that comforted my aching heart.

"Must we make him grow up so quickly?" she asked, smiling.

"He was never given the choice, Melitta. And though the happiness surrounds him now, we need to give him a shield for when the demons of his soul come. I know these fiends all too well, and I shudder thinking what would've happened to me if I had not the tools to deal with these hardships."

"And yet, your soul pains you now."

"For other reasons."

"Will there ever be a day where it does not?"

"I fear not. But I shall still search for it."

"Just promise me one thing, my love," she pleaded with me. "Only do what is needed. Do not attempt desperate glory. It will not win my heart; that is already yours. Do your job, and when your job is done, come home to us. I care not for valor or glory, only for you."

"If I do my job correctly, neither of these will I need to call upon."

"Is it always the way of the world, that good leaders suffer so much personal heartache?"

I thought of Achilles, and Chrysanthe. His passion for heroism and her passion for heroes told a far different story than ours.

"I avoid thoughts such as these, my love." Lying through my teeth. She always knew when I did not tell her the entirety of my sorrow.

"You, of all people, Stelios, do not avoid thinking of these things…" But she let the topic slide. For the rest of the evening, we watched as our boy played in the river, and picked up sticks just to break them, as children do. That night we tucked his warm little body into bed, and my rough fingertips tightened the linen underneath his back. He drifted off into a deep sleep.

We were to leave for the trials under the cover of darkness but upon a calm sea. This type of voyage would represent the change in the boys, and we would implore them to sit in silence and not only reflect, but, just as importantly, imagine a future version of themselves that they could be proud of.

I spoke to them as my old mentors loaded and prepared the boats.

"We will help you become men, even if your minds cannot conceive it at this time, but be certain of one thing." I paused. "We do not give out our black armor easily."

"We earn the scars we wear."

As the boat rocked on the waves, and the stars took their rightful place as the watchers of the earth and of us, my son approached, sat beside me, and silently watched the sea as I did. I knew he had something to say, but I would not push him to do so, for these children needed to gain the confidence to speak to adults as adults. The crashing sea filled the silence.

"I remember."

"The sea has carried it to you?" I inquired.

"No, Father — the gods above have. On this night, I lifted my gaze to the stars. All my life it was low. But then I remembered the stars above. They stand sentry over my heart. It is by their hand that I survived my past, and now, I remember. They spoke to me on this fine night…

"I am Odysseus." The waves seemed to shudder beneath the ship.

"Odysseus," I repeated. "I wish I knew the meaning of the name."

"It means '*son of pain.*'"

The clouds ripped across the overwhelming sky we travelled beneath. They brought the darkness. The abyss of the night terrifies children and brings forth monsters that only they may see, but it became a personal tool, a shield, a spear-tip, for Odysseus to harness in order to build himself into a man. There was a power within him. I could see in his eyes that he yearned to live. Before Melitta and Odysseus, I spent most days wishing to die.

He could be a man who embraced all of his existence, despite the brutality of his upbringing. The boy faced with courage the one thing life had always denied him. That was true living, and true mettle in the face of tremendous adversity.

I said nothing but put my arm across his shoulders. It was in that moment, Zeus, as the salted spray from the ocean landed in cold droplets upon my arm, that I first understood that such titles as "father" or "son" are not granted by birthright, but rather earned by actions.

The days I spent commanding the operation were much like the days I spent as a trainee. What I realized was that though I constantly made mistakes, the boys never noticed. Every mistake was a chance to maneuver. Each unintended action had unintended positives we could extract. War is much the same.

There is a misconception among men that rank, and experience, for that matter, provide confidence in leaders — the truth is much simpler. All people in a position of power are to a certain degree pretending they know more than they actually do.

I took pride in watching the boy grow, and in developing my own teaching style, which differed from many of the officers' in the regiment. I found much hope in my honesty, and I found my men capable of executing their duties without much need of my interjections. In short, I trusted them, and since they witnessed my actions of trust, they trusted me in return.

No leader whose actions do not follow his words is worth his salt. In his mind he may lead, but in the hearts of his men those fracture lines will appear. The men will at first obediently but begrudgingly carry out his will, but deep down their aggravations will fester like insects who gather upon a rotting body. This problem begins in peace; in the chaos and terror of war these aggravations will push to a boiling point, and men will die as a result. The leader then has two choices, of which he will only pick one, for he has inculcated himself in his own dogma and proven that his ego is worth more to him than lives. He will not back down. He will choose to hammer down his previous narrow-sighted orders, instead of taking a step back to analyze the complexities and the dangers.

Because he has chosen pride, he will always choose pride, and in peace the consequences are minor, but in war they are destructive.

This is not a story of war. It is the story of the apparent things we do wrong, and continue to do wrong, despite their obvious poison to our lives — it is because we are human and because we are flawed to our cores. But, because we are mortal, and our lives fleeting, the knowledge of the right thing to do, and the knowledge that our lives are over in moments, tears us apart, so we walk the fine line between passion and mortality. But when we fall, we fall drastically, with violence. Those who cannot hold this fine line often stumble, and their lives collapse completely.

But, if we do hold, we are often left wondering of what we missed out on, and what passions we might never had experienced because we set our sights too far from passion. In leadership, as in life, the choice is the same. An officer cannot rip the passion away from the task at hand — it does not sit well in the hearts of men whose passions fire from their infallible spirit. On the other side, if a leader acts only on emotion, his choices will not consider the entirety of the situation. His rising blood, his bubbling passion, will often result in the wrong choice, and the loss of trust of his men.

When I returned to Thessaly, just before the trials were about to begin, years had passed. I had visited my wife as much as I possibly could during this time. I recounted all of Odysseus' failures and successes, and we reveled in his growth. We still wished for a younger sibling for our already growing boy, but the gods would not grant us one. Our lives were still complete, and I thought seriously about leaving the army at that point. I brought the topic up while Melitta and I strolled through the forest.

"I want for nothing more than to be a father," I said.

She looked confused. "That which you already are, Stelios."

"A true father, who does not leave his sons and daughters constantly for war."

She looked at me sternly. "A soldier must do his job. But if you leave, then leave entirely. Break free from that piece of your mind, because if you leave in your mind, but not in your body, you will die. Or, worse, you will lose focus in war, and others will die, which will break you further."

"And you would still love me if I were no longer a Myrmidon? You would love a coward whose armor sits atop the hill?" I asked, not genuinely wanting the answer. But she surprised me.

"You honestly believe I care what profession you have, don't you? You think so little of me? I care not for armor, or for titles. I respect and love everything you've done for your country and your men, but I would love you even if you shoveled pig shit for a living, and smelled to the gods at the end of the day."

"You joke, my love, but I have done that exact thing as a slave, and it is not as glamorous as it may sound."

"Regardless. I love you for who you are, and not what you've done in your profession. I love you for how deeply you see the world, its faults, and its goodness. Leave the army, if you will, but do so with the knowledge that I am with you whatever direction our lives take."

"Here lies the problem, my love. I know not who I am without them. To lay my armor down means to start anew. I know not my soul. All I know is war. What shall I do, if I do decide to leave the only thing I've ever truly known and been proud of in my life?"

She stopped on the trail. She said, honestly and sincerely, "You shall listen to that which, above all, guides you. You must listen to your heart."

I looked deeply into her eyes.

"She has already spoken."

I ran my hand through the silk of her hair.

With the trials concluded and my decision made, I was at peace with the end of my time in black. I saw in the eyes of the boys that I had not condemned them to a life of war, but rather given them what they desperately needed. It was not my place to decide for them, but rather to provide what tools I could, and let each boy choose for himself how best to deal with the harshness of existence.

I was set to leave what I had known my whole life. It unshackled the chains that had been weighing heavily upon my chest. And when we returned, we did so with proficient men, in all but experience. Men who stood ready and willing to take on the suffering that life so evidently is, and to carry the burden that I no longer could.

The sky was almost completely engulfed in darkness when we arrived. But as we landed on the beach, at our home, our place of peace, something had changed in the Myrmidons. Some unease was evident. Our ships lay barren, absent of guards or weapons. Some floated without lashing. They now drifted lifelessly, absent of soldiers in the littoral waters. A conflict brewed. An unexplained void.

A Myrmidon walked the beach, drunk and kicking pieces of old gear. I recognized him as Hypatios, the man with great intellect. As he passed beside me, I could see in him the image of the boy he used to be. Instead of contracting with laughter, his swollen, red eyes did not even acknowledge my presence. Instead of short, shining brown hair, it was long, dirty, and unkept. No words were exchanged between us. He walked away into the night down the lonely beach.

"Men," I addressed the ship of new warriors, "have this beach cleaned when I return." The young soldiers nodded. The older ones, Deimos, Teris, and Iesos, looked worriedly at me. They sensed some insidious temperament as well.

Because all teams are a result of their leaders, it was immediately clear to me that something must be wrong with Achilles, and so, I sought him out at my earliest opportunity.

IX

A LINE DIVIDING EACH HEART

I did not see him until the next morning. I spent the night tossing under the sheets, unable to find sleep. Early at dawn, I went to the shores to wait for him, but when I arrived, I found him already sitting alone atop a washed-up tree. I saw his blonde hair and his reflection on the ocean, calm below the rising sun. When Achilles heard me approach, he turned begrudgingly towards me, as if I were a summer insect he had to flick from his shoulder. Unlike before, long ago on the same beach, his turn did not match the aggression required for the moment. His eyes did not lower with determination, but rather they narrowed with a look of villainy. I feared he could no longer control the monster inside him — it enveloped him and lashed out at me. It flourished, like a weed, with each passing moment that the hate filled his heart.

"Tell me friend, what dismay has occurred here?" I began.

He shook his head angrily and kicked the hard sand. "The soldiers prepare for war."

"What war? What soldiers?" I demanded. "These men look like regulars at the tavern. Garbage and filth stain the beach."

"They are soldiers. Who cares? They fight and screw and drink. They are beasts of war. I shall do nothing but turn them loose on the foe."

I looked around, scanned, and only then did I notice the void that had ripped apart our home.

Sickness. It had taken a huge portion of the village. A mass funeral pyre was dug into the Thessalian earth over the ridge, and the ashes lay dormant upon the green grass that flowed in the wind. Houses sat in rubble. Memorial stones lined the hills. And where were the two people in this world who could have held this man together? Chrysanthe would not put up with such unheroic behavior. His son would not look up to such a father.

"Where are they...? Achilles. Where are they?!" I demanded. "What have you done with them? Sent them away? Discarded them? Tell me the truth in this moment!"

He seethed; the words came like venom at me from his mouth. He clasped a broken mug in his hand. I recognized it as the tea used for our training. He took another swig.

"They are gone! Do not mention their names to me. I do not need their grace or their memories. I do not want their useless pain. It aids me not. A man can only take what is his in this life. I will kill. I have always known killing. I will define my life by taking others. And I will kill Hector. His ability has caused rumblings in Greece. I will crush these rumors so viciously and with such anger... all of Greece will know that Achilles was a warrior of history!"

"What meaning is this, 'gone'?" I asked, confused. Achilles was rambling, and the violence in his voice made me uncomfortable. In my mind, I worried for my own wife.

He turned towards me, the sun separating our bodies on the sand.

"You have no business in prodding. Your job is to shut up, listen, and execute, or risk the mutinous penalty of death." He took another drink of the mixture held in his right hand.

"You aren't the man I've known," I pleaded.

"That man was weak, subject to the whims of the gods. He was subject to care for family. That is no warrior life. The leader of the Myrmidons cannot be weak. He cannot care about anything other than war, and warriors. If I show weakness, the snakes will emerge from our ranks. I do not trust them already. They look from the corner of their eyes with helpless ambition. They want my position and my power."

"The men want nothing," I answered, "only the promise that was made before. The Myrmidons would only fight for that which they believed in. They fought for injustice and for the eradication of the pain of those not strong enough to fight it themselves."

"And even still! We risk, and we sacrifice, and we die, and no matter how many we save, the things we love are still taken! That which we strive for is nothing but a farce! A hopeless pursuit! I want blood for my pain. I will take everything from the gods. I will take blood for blood. Body for body. And at every funeral procession and in the minds of all those who lost, they will know the name 'Achilles.'"

He was avoiding the truth at all costs. Finally, I snapped with his insolence. I grabbed his shoulders hard, like he had done with mine back in Rhodes. "Where are they!?" I screamed in his face.

For a moment shock filled his face, and it brought him down from his drunken heights.

"I tried to save them," he said quietly. "I fed them. I brought fresh water to their bedside each hour. I scoured the hills for the herbs and vines the healers needed. I did not sleep." His hands began to shake. His voice rose with the gale.

"I watched as they withered and died! I held their hands in death, and I prayed to the gods. I was given no answer! No justification! Nothing! I curse the gods where they stand. I implored the great god Zeus to fight me where I stood! I would rip his pathetic existence to pieces and feed it to the wolves. The gods, ha! What cowards. What insolent, scheming, vile, vicious beasts. They ripped my beating heart from my chest."

His voice was not torn by sadness, as it should have been. It was wrought with anger and it flowed from his mouth as he spit his venom at me. The tempest of his rage ripped his soul into fragmented pieces. His tired eyes scanned his flanks for enemies.

How was I to comfort a father and husband?

Sickness is imperceptible, free from purpose, and in its arbitrary choice of men, women, and children alike, it gives no indication of why. But Achilles was the only man who raged so deeply. I witnessed the other fathers, husbands, sons, and daughters who lost, and they did not turn as he did; they did not curse the heavens, nor foam with intense anger. Grieving and weeping, they mourned their losses.

Achilles was ready to tear the world to pieces over his.

He broke with the knowledge that it must have been some higher power who chose them for death. He blamed the gods. He blamed you, Zeus.

This was not the strong, golden-haired man I knew. I found a broken man, shattered beyond all recognition, who had lost the path of the warrior, lost his will, and in his disillusionment with the cruelty of fate, lost his direction. His soul, driven by war and compounded by hate, turned black and violent.

His lungs heaved. The sweat, glistening in the Grecian sunshine was beading from above his right brow. His eyes no longer held the color of the Aegean as they once had. They were black, like the experienced and angry warriors who had seen too much death. But they were not the stoic black of our armor, nor the expansive black of the night over the mountains. They were the black of hell, of the abyss.

His black eyes burned into me. Achilles' right hand tightly gripped the handle of his sword.

"To war then, for I have known no other life with you." My voice had wavered but I fooled him enough. His grip loosened.

Achilles, unable to see past his ruin, had grasped the only thing he had left. He was a student of war. Unmatched throughout our ranks, his ability to murder was astounding. And so, like Narcissus, the books of history would not read of a broken man, but rather a ruthless warrior. But in his desperate search, he was willing to sacrifice all his men, including my son and me.

I left him there on the beach, staring out over the ocean. The same sand we grew up on now turned its back on him. He now stood on the beach with his immense arrogance and hate for the world.

There I was, torn between my responsibilities as a husband and father, and my dedication to Achilles and to my men. Did I have a choice but to act, knowing it could result in his death, or mine, but with the knowledge that I could save my son and my wife?

Is a leader nothing but self-sacrificing? Is a father not the same?

Our professions did not make the world simpler. In truth, our positions only further complicated life, and left me lost trying to mandate my passions and goals of family, legacy, and service. But I also knew that in that ruin of Achilles and in the hearts of our men, the very darkness of which we sought to rid the world of in the first place could rear its monstrous head. The consequences would be far more devastating.

It is difficult to live the right way. It is easy to die. It is also much harder to live a long life with integrity than it is to discard it completely, and to lose all touch with humanity. I knew the world would forever know his name, but there is much more than fame to live for in this life.

"I did not blame him, for we lived our lives in the pursuit of the gods, and yet, they appeared as the only ones to blame for the tragedies he endured."

Zeus spoke, *"The reasons for this will be explained, Myrmidon. Know only that not all men are as faultless as yourself. They corrupt."*

"It is fine for a man to hurt, and to grieve for the loss of love, but if he does not recover, he will find himself in the depths of his self-made despair, never to rise from the abyss from which he has placed himself."

He would not recover from this pain.

Because our leader had compromised his morals and ethics, it was not long until that poisonous drip seeped from the downfall of Achilles and treacherously found its way to the group. I cannot recount to you the horror that began to form. Soon, we lived in a tribal state, where we locked our doors at night, and we snaked through the streets undetected. I had to get my family out. It was no place for good souls.

My life, then, was also not worth the death of countless future soldiers. My wife was strong, my son brave and fearless; I would miss them with all my heart. But at the end of all things, I knew that I must convince Achilles of his impending glory, of his everlasting legacy. I must convince him to war, in order to help him fall. I had to do this; I would face the venom in the blackening hearts of men and what horrors they could truly impose on the world when the leash severed.

Facing me was the choice to either be complicit or die a cowards' death — to place my armor on the hill.

The men we had just trained were new; Achilles did not yet poison them. I enlisted the help of my three mentors to shuffle them safely from the island that night. "Goodbye, my dear friends," I told them. "The Myrmidons are no more. I fear that we shall all perish in battle. Do not worry for the rage of Achilles. He, and the others, in this state, will not notice your absence. I cannot thank you enough for your service to me, and to the true memory of the ant-men."

"Let us stay and destroy these cowards!" barked Deimos angrily, though he struggled to raise his shield. His age betrayed his courage.

"To stay is certain death, my friend, and it is not a sentence I shall condemn you to. Take the men, return to the island for the supplies and tents that remain there, and wait for me, and my family. Before the spring sun rises, I shall meet you there, and we shall create a new life for ourselves.

All of you must go, in case the Myrmidons come for the boys. Protect them with your lives," I pleaded.

Iesos spoke. "Zeus shall guide us and protect your family, my friend."

"He speaks through you, Iesos," I replied, and I hugged each man as a sibling. "Odysseus will stay with me for a moment. I have need to speak to my son before he leaves this place. I will bring him to you at the training ground when we sail from this forsaken place."

Therefore, the choice now left to me was simple. I knew then I could leave the Myrmidons, and I knew that in my absence, many more would die, good and evil men alike. And yet, if I went to war with him, I knew I would die, as the sole reason for my participation would be to save as many of the men as I could, the ones Achilles had not corrupted.

Either way, I faced death, but in the great balance of all life, it was my life or theirs. And if I stayed, I knew for certain that the faces of the men and the faces of their wives and children would haunt me for the rest of eternity.

And I thought I knew sacrifice before parenthood, but I had no such clue. I had to save my son. I had to save all the sons of all the good men, whom Achilles might have otherwise destroyed. For as powerful as hope can be, it is clear that when we lose hope its absence can be just as damaging and disparaging to the temperaments of young men.

I could not live with the world with this Achilles in it, and I knew the rest of the Myrmidons would not mutiny against the man who gave them exactly what drove their primal desires. I could only rely on the few men I trusted. If I failed, Achilles would take us all to a pointless war to die, all in the pursuit of his own glory.

In the solitude of my mind, I could see the now blue eyes of my son, like the calm waters of the Aegean on a summer morning. Not black, and rough like mine, and like Achilles' were now. Yes, we thought we knew sacrifice before we became parents, when we gave everything for each other in training, but this was different, and yet very much the same because I was comfortable with the end of my life for something superior.

It is astounding that despite all the grandeur and the unreachable and boundless frontiers of the great world, in all the endless mountains and valleys and the deepest parts of the vast oceans, and the devastating power of the storms and of the volcanoes, on the wind and in the wilderness of the heavens that watch over us and all the insignificance of everything we are and will ever be within these things, the objects of greatest consequence in our lives are such small human beings.

But do we give in, or do we hold on with the limits of our grit, and trudge, painfully, through the pits of our lives, in the hopes we leave behind something better? Do we save those who deserve it more than we do? Do we die knowing that instead of cowardice, we reached back and pulled a dying soul from the flame? Such is our lives. Principles are simple; living by them has never been so.

The answer was clear to me, and it is now, even in death. I could not rely on war. Battle would not be enough to stop him. Achilles, the man he had become, my old friend, had fallen victim to his most vile natures and most base instincts. To save them, the man had to die.

X

ASK US NOT HOW WE LIVED, BUT HOW WE DIED

This meant saying goodbye to those I loved the most. By the time I challenged this man, the white of their sails needed to reach far beyond the horizon. Knowing his fury, and his now contemptible spirit, the last thing I could risk was his sword turning its scorn towards my family.

I put my trust in the only man I had left. The lion. The last of the Myrmidons whose character I still knew deeply, and whose blaze still burned with mine. My son was still young, and the youth needed the guidance of men whose lives were altered by war, but who, like me, felt their essences fracture from it. I found Leandros on the point of rocks that lined the beach. He sat atop the edge of the crescent moon bay, the same one that had one held our hopes firm in its hands, and now whose waters looked black to us.

I requested from him one final favor. "My old friend, if you have it within you, I must ask the worst thing possible of you…" And because he was a true Myrmidon, a true man of courage, Leandros, whom I was proud to call my ally, replied before I could even explain what needed to be done.

"Anything," he said, without hesitation. "With the gods as my witness, Stelios, ask of me anything in this moment, and I shall do it for you." Leandros craved with every piece of his being a redemption from what we had become.

"Delay your armor its final resting place upon the hill." I pointed to the oaken ship, primed and eager to meet the sea again. Atop stood the shadowy figures of my wife and child.

He understood. "Where shall I take them?"

"Take them to where the sun still gleams across the sea, where the rain still lingers crisp and cold in the morning, and where they might find salvation and harmony with the world, as we once knew but which seems so distant to us now."

"Can I not do more? Can I not confront his dark heart with you?"

I looked at the man and patted him on the back. "You have stayed with me till the very end, my brother. That in itself is the most heroic act. Our mentors are not the warriors they once were; my family will need a lion. They will need protection."

"But when we leave, my friend, what will you be left with?" he asked.

I looked into the brown eyes of my love, whose hand clasped and interlaced with that of the black-armored man's, my son, both of whom I loved so deeply, with such a blaze that, as long as they lived, would ignite my endless soul.

"Peace." As I said the word and believed it, the fractured pieces of my heart, which I had left buried throughout the world with the dead men, returned at once to Thessaly. The pieces nestled deep and serenely in the gentle chests of my family, where they slept softly upon feathered pillows, resting, finally.

I approached my family on the deck of the ship. Their lives, now packed into small satchels, lined the rope canvas of the vessel. The rocks that lined the shores behind us sat layered and jagged, but in the shadow of the sun as it balanced its edge upon the horizon, they drafted a tender story upon the hillside. For a moment, the world sat level, and in balance, until the sun dipped beyond the sea, indicating that my time had come.

I put my hand on Odysseus' shoulder and looked deep into his eyes, which were now filled with sky blue. "There are no true partings for a father and son, for that which dies within me shall flourish within you. For that reason and many others, I shall always be with you." I turned him towards the bow of the ship, leaned over his shoulder, and whispered, "Your aim shall follow your eyes. Always turn them towards the stars, and you shall always be brave, my son. They shall take their leave from this day onward, and it shall be I who watches. When you need me, be not afraid to ask the gods."

I kissed him on the forehead, and gently turned him away from death. That was the only action required from a father who wished to lead his child towards the light. Melitta looked at me, and with tears in her eyes she kissed my rough face.

"Farewell, my heart," she said.

"Whatever awaits me now, I shall find you again. I carry you with me, my love, and no longer am I afraid. If the gods grant us but one more life, I shall spend each second staring at you."

I touched her soft skin for the final time.

The white sails filled in the breeze, and, watching from the lonely shores, I lingered long in the darkness, as my family pursued the sun.

As I turned, I steeled my gaze and knelt down to pick up a handful of sand. The grit made its way to the creases in my palms and fingers. I gripped it tight and looked skyward to the starry sky where the constellations of the gods shone, and from where I knew my judgement would come. Silently I prayed to them.

Achilles was sitting in the courtyard, below the hanging baskets that held so many of my heartfelt memories. Fully equipped with his black armor, he turned his head as I entered the stone-laden enclosure.

"No man deserves to die for the glory of Achilles," I said to him.

"Soldiers die. Such is war. Commanders are remembered, certainly, but the name 'Achilles' will be etched in stone. It will ring in the ears of every widow and son who will forever know their men were not strong enough for this world. Victory goes only to the strong and ruthless."

"As does damnation, and eternal fire."

"Put down your sword, Stelios, before you get hurt."

"Pick up yours, before death comes for you," I replied.

His eyes narrowed. He slowly stood up while adjusting the handle of his shield. "You will need more than courage for this fight, I fear. Half of me is that which you cannot kill."

"Then my blade seeks the other half. The half who so pathetically fell to the ground as I slammed his shield so long ago. I should have killed you then. You lose yourself now, Achilles; look at your armor."

He wore shining black armor, newly refinished at the hands of a blacksmith. He had erased his scars, and forgotten all of his memories, burned by the fires of the forge. "You forget who you are, and what we are."

He circled me, and I moved with his threat. The cobbled stones sat uneven, but my feet felt aware of the imbalance and compensated. He spoke.

"And yet here we are, brothers destined to meet, and to send one of our souls to the depths."

"If my soul goes to the dungeons of Tartarus for this act of treason," I spat, "then I'm afraid it merely waits for yours there, old friend, for you have also condemned yourself to the hanging chains."

Achilles lunged. I blocked his first left-handed strike with my shield. The echo rang through the town. The wood from the shutters of the windows clanged against the stone. He lunged again, darting to my left. I ducked the first overhead glance, and with my sword directed the returning blow to my right as the sparks from the metal flew into the night. I felt hot blood on the top of my shoulder. A glance, but a hit regardless.

"These are no broomstick handles," he said.

My breathing quickened. The adrenaline in my veins soared. I took a step with the left foot towards him and lifted my shield up to block his vision as I swung with my right. He turned his left palm towards the ground and parried, but as he lingered, I caught him with the piece of violence he knew so well. I brought the tip of the lifted shield down with a crack onto the back of his collar above the shoulder blades.

He pivoted and jumped back to his feet enraged. He came at me wildly. An overhead I blocked, along with a low twist, but he caught me with the broad side of his shield, which slammed me backwards and stole the air from my lungs. I heaved and coughed.

The rage fueled him now. He came at me with a broad stroke, left hand to the neck. As I ducked, I felt my toes catch the edge of a mislaid stone. Some mason had made a mistake in history that now saved my life, and I pushed underneath the blow and swiveled to catch him from the back. Achilles was unbelievably fast, however, and at my full I merely scratched his armor.

He looked shocked. Some recognition of mortality struck him. He turned his right heel and watched as the blood poured into the joints between the stones. The fire in his eyes extinguished, and his wild strikes transformed into heavy breathing and worry. He shook his head clear.

He lowered his sword to his hip. "You know, I wonder why it is, Stelios, you find yourself here all alone. No friends, no comrades show their faces to back your cause." He paused. "Have you ever asked yourself why?"

I remained silent.

"Was it not your order that killed Alexius? Shame. Such a talented man. Does he not visit you in your dreams? Does he not curse you from Elysium for your poor leadership? The officer, and friend, who got him killed. He haunts you, no?"

His laughing image shattered the confines of my battle-hardened mind. His smile flickered with the dying torches on the wall in front of me.

"And Kalliaros? Years of combat he survived, and yet he died alongside you, far from the fields of war. Were you not the man charged with guarding his flank? Was it not your job to secure his flank? How many more of your friends have died for your sins? How many lives was it worth? How many of your brothers need to die while you justify war?"

The linen-wrapped body of my friend appeared on the stones. Blood stained the white marble.

"It was solely your fault they died, old friend. You own their deaths with every breath you take. I'll do you the honor of taking such a burden away from you."

I could not see Achilles anymore, only their lost faces. Their deaths were mine to bear. No children, nor wives would ever see them again, and each painful minute in each shattering second of the lives of their loved ones was sitting on my shoulders. My eyes clouded with tears. I swung wildly around the courtyard, with nothing but pain and suffering as my guide.

Achilles took his chance. As I desperately lunged with my right hand he twisted and pinned my arm inside his shield. Completing the pirouette of death, he rammed the tip of his sword through my chest with such force that the metal of my back armor shattered and sprinkled atop the stones as the weapon exited my body.

In the brief moments I had left, I thought of my companions. I thought of the soft hair cascading to the shoulders of Melitta, and my son, whose eyes restored more color each day, and I prayed to the gods for the salvation of Achilles. If there was any hope left in this world, I hoped for him to just return to the quiet, blonde-haired boy, sat quietly in the corner of a ship. I dropped to my knees and waited to die.

"I s-saw you — your eyes, that first night. So long ago, when you were uncorrupted."

He was silent. His chest heaved with rage.

"In… the … darkness… I saw your fear…. It was…the same as… mine…" I gasped for air, but blood filled my lungs instead. With a final push of strength, I uttered my last words, through the pain of his sword, which remained plunged into my chest.

"It is... what made us men... Its absence... is what ... now... makes us monsters."

This is not a story of war, though the consequences of war were ever-present. It is a story of what we must withstand — the storm that rages for us and us alone, so that in our ultimate moments, when we find ourselves engulfed in the heat of the blaze, we find the courage to hold the ground we stand upon.

And here now I find myself at Olympus. The amount of time which elapsed between death and now, I know nothing of. I know not how long I was climbing this mountain. All I remember, from the very end, was the darkness and the feeling of steel tearing through the muscles of my chest. And in my last moment, I saw her face.

Finally, I found peace.

XI

STILL WATERS BENEATH

Zeus looked down upon the man as the warrior concluded his tale, and the Myrmidon addressed the great god directly.

"Did he ever have a choice?" the warrior asked of Achilles.

Zeus answered, *"All men have choices. His was to have glory above all. In death, his only wish was for his downfall to shine far above the successes of other men."*

"Did we ever have a choice?" asked the Myrmidon.

Zeus sat back in his throne, his eyebrows lowered towards the soldier. *"How did you live, Myrmidon? Did the joys of your life align with the joys of his? What victories in life will you carry to the next? Are they memories of war and war alone?"*

"The victories are not solely mine. I never accomplished them alone," said the man. "Life is nothing if it is not lived for ones who bird your soul together. We won, because we carried the weight of our discomfort, fostered our friendships, and loved the ones who loved us back. We sat beside the sea, and the rivers, and the white-tipped mountains, and we truly breathed in the moments given to us. Unlike the gods, we did not see life as never-ending; we saw it as a gift that could be given as quickly as taken away. In the end and in our own way, we retained our morality."

Zeus watched the man. The warrior's tears fell silently on the stones of the great hall of Olympus. The man's head stayed bowed. He was imprisoned to the depths of his pain.

"Before I leave, would the great god Zeus permit me to ask what became of him?"

Zeus nodded, but he remained silent.

Stelios' agony burst forth. "Why did you have to take them from him?" he pleaded. "Had he not suffered enough? My friend… His heart was fraught with the pains of his life."

"We do not control the outcomes of man, Myrmidon. We are bound to watch from the shadows of the mountain, but we exist as an outlet to blame, so mortals at least have names to curse. But Achilles would not settle for blame; his heart blackened despite using us as his escape for suffering. It was in this moment that I cursed my creation and knew that my ideals had been put to the test, and they had failed."

Zeus bowed his head, and a noticeable pain came across his face. *"You asked Achilles to step down, at the right moment, and he walked along the tributary that night, near the shining town, and contemplated his loss of power. The world is cruel. He convinced himself that he would never abdicate his position. Long before the cracks in his character were revealed to you, the tyrant began to brew in his soul."*

"Why then have you summoned me here, Zeus? If you knew that your creation caused such incredible heartache? Why do my hands still ache from the rocks of the slope you summoned me to climb?

Zeus considered this and nodded. *"Yes, Myrmidon, I know the depths of the terror I caused. Like you, it haunts me in the night. You truly want to know why you are here, and not him, the man who scorned us both?"*

"Before the long night takes me, I do."

"You are here because we took the same things from you as we stole from him: love, fatherhood, and happiness. We took them just as brutally as we did from Achilles, but from a far less corrupt man in yourself. So let me ask you this: why do you not

curse me where I stand as he did? Why was it that your soul did not turn to black? How does a man consciously say goodbye to the things he loves the most, in order to save them? How did you withstand the storm, in the moments where you should have surely crumbled, as he did?" He paused. "The gods cannot change what happens in the world of men. They can merely presume, create, and hope their conceptions stand the test of fate, and when mine failed to do so, I was prisoner to watching its horrific events unfold. All the terrible things that happened were my shackles, and they bound my heart for eternity next to the other desperations we spoke of. I summoned you here because you deserve the truth."

Zeus stepped down from his marble throne, and in doing so, he appeared to the Myrmidon the size of a man. Zeus put his hand on the warrior's shoulder.

"I beckoned you here because I find myself in a position of which no man has put me in before — I envy your character, and yet I am the cause of your heartache. I, who slew the almighty Kronos, who cast down the titans, I, who commands the pantheon, envy a mere man. I summoned you here because, at the culmination of your life and at the end of your time with me, and, granted by the gods, you asked me for one question. You... you asked about his pain, and not your own. That, my son, is why you are here upon the mountain. Why, in regard to your own suffering and loss, do you seek no answer?"

Bowing his head, Stelios stared at the plaster that held the stones below his feet together. It was clean at the joints.

"The answer frightens me beyond measure. I carry it with me, forever... I carry them in my heart. The heaviest of all things..."

"They are not far, my friend, as those we love as never far from our hearts. Your story shall be one more I add to the desperations of my soul, and for that, brave warrior, I shall be eternally remorseful. He who has taught the gods what it means to be divine, take your leave. They are not here, Myrmidon. But they are closer than it may seem.

"Your wife brought him to an island in the realm of the living — she raised Odysseus to be kind and valiant. Your three mentors joined them. They were old men, but they taught the boy to be wise and clever, and to not fall victim to the failures of warriors. The men you admired died having found that which they searched for their *entire lives — peace."*

A look of happiness appeared on the soldier's face for the first time since meeting the god.

Zeus continued.

"But you cannot see them now, for you have passed over. The golden fields await you. Kalliaros sits there, with his love, Elenia. They picnic and drink wine made from the vines of Thessaly. Your friends laugh in the sunlight. Their expressions crinkle with joy as Alexius jokes with them. And, with the sun cast behind them, they tell stories of you, and they all sit together, waiting patiently to see your figure appear above the shining hill."

"Follow that which guides you, soldier."

"I am saddened I missed his life. A father's job is to be present, to embrace his son, and to reassure him that everything will be alright, even when in his heart, he knows this to be false."

"Your son lives, indeed, and he is a hero among men. He has a remarkable story still to recount, one which will drive the hearts of men for generations. He may be the last hope for us, the gods. He was certainly the last hope for Achilles. Without him, our flames might have already extinguished forever. But when I am done with him, I shall send him straight into your arms, to embrace you among the fields. Of all the things I have failed to grant you, Stelios, this promise I shall keep."

A crack of lightning tore through the hall. Blinding light filled the temple, and the Myrmidon turned his head and covered his eyes. The stones surrounding the Myrmidon severed and frayed, and the god of war, Ares, who he had met so long ago, appeared once more to the man, standing in the corner of the halls of Olympus. No longer did the armor of Ares glimmer. His cape fluttered in the wind, still bearing the crimson of his battle colors, but tattered and old. His long hair had turned ancient. He was not the young god who had visited the Myrmidon so long ago.

Ares arrived before the Myrmidon and grabbed him by both shoulders.

"The time is now, brother."

Departing together, they walked past the throne of Zeus, deep into the temple of the gods. Stelios held his head high, and his back straight. Ares draped his powerful arm over the man's shoulder, in comfort. Stelios felt like a boy again.

These soldiers, these brothers in arms, walked in unison. Their steps echoed throughout the great halls. The Myrmidon left with dignity, and with happiness, and with an understanding that all of the pain he'd endured was for the sake of everyone he cared for. Heavy in his hand was the torch he carried, the one he bore for those he loved.

Not once in his life had the flame extinguished.

Ares led him to the river. When he saw the white sails on the horizon, his heart held apprehension, for he no longer had possession of his coin. But as the swaying ship approached, he saw that it was not Charon coming to ferry him across the river of the dead; it was a man whom he'd known well in life. A lion of a man. Still, in death, Leandros faithfully sailed the ship. He had come to deliver the final piece of the Myrmidon's heart to the fields.

Ares spoke to him with a voice like fire. "Though our wars are long, our moments are short. Take this moment for yourself, young soldier, and find peace." The god carried Stelios' tattered helmet in his left hand. And, as the God of War turned to leave, Stelios saw each scar clearly. In each mark he saw a moment where, if not for his helmet or his brothers, he would have died.

Certain now that his loved ones waited for him, the warrior breathed a sigh of relief. With his last step, Stelios climbed aboard the oaken craft. Upon his back, he felt the heat of the torches that lined the hall, and a warmth which he had not felt in ages guided him towards those who he had loved and lost.

He could feel her close now.

Leandros and Stelios sailed across the stormy river. The shoreline soon came into view. Stalks of wheat moved in the wind. And, in the distance, Stelios could see shadows resting among golden fields.

Each shadow stood as they noticed the approaching ship.

Three old mentors, battle ready.

A joker.

A leader.

And a woman.

But no son.

She ran towards the coast with the others not far behind. Stelios' heartbeat quickened and the blood surged through his veins, but for once, it was not the anticipation of battle that gripped his spirit. He jumped from the ship into the shallow water and trudged through the cold towards them, but something stopped him. The river flowed around his ankles, but the warrior froze in place. His tears fell into the river.

The golden sun, rays breaking into fractured light, dipped behind the Myrmidon and cast a shadow across the warm sand and ebbing tide. His eyes slowly shut.

After the eternity that was Stelios' life, something inside him finally broke loose. It was the ineffable thing that all soldiers carried inside them. Gifted to them by the God of War, Ares, it lay hidden deep in the caverns of their hearts. It was not strength, nor aggression, nor tactics, nor any of the things taught by war. It was woven in bone and weaved into muscle. It was a steel plate, like a shield. And hidden far below the surface, it gave soldiers the ability to carry the most painful of things, when all others would break.

But it was time to let it go.

As he loosened his clenched fists, a piece of the soldier drifted down slowly beneath the waves, and he finally felt free. He knew he was free because although he could not see her, he could feel her lips close to his, hanging in the air only a breath away.

And as his feet fell upon dry land, his eyes opened, but the man who opened his eyes was not the same one who had closed them. His body remained the same, but his eyes had aged with time. They became still like the calm ocean in the morning breeze as they met hers.

He embraced the ones he had loved in life.

Turning back towards the shore, with her in his arms, Stelios stared across the endless horizon. White crests curling atop the waves slowed the very fabric of time. He realized then that it was no longer the grit and bravery that defined him as a soldier that would bring his son home; rather, it was the immovability and endurance of a father's patience. But in his heart, he knew that he would see Odysseus soon, and this granted him peace.

And for the first time, he understood the other side of war.

Back in the hall, between the pillars, a man lingered in the shadows. He had listened to the warrior's tale. Between the creases of his palms was dried and crusted white plaster. The mason leaned against one of the pillars of the earth. After a deep contemplation for the things he had heard, the mason stepped out into the light, and Zeus turned his gaze.

"Homer," he said, addressing the mason. "Paint this man as he was in life. Valiant, noble, tough, and full of heartache. Men should read these pillars and strive for such bravery in life. But Homer, leave one pillar bare."

Zeus settled back into his seat, and as he set his arms down on the edges of his rock throne, the tips of his fingers froze and turned to stone. Travelling through his arms and his feet the unyielding stone took the form of where his robes flowed last in the wind. It enveloped his chest. Drifting through his fractured heart and as his figure hardened upon the throne of marble, the stone captured his pained expression; stooped in sorrow, his head bowed. Until the next summoned warrior would arrive at the pinnacle of the world, Zeus, God of Thunder and Ruler of Olympus, was still. And from his throne, sealed in his resting place, he waited.

The mason nodded. Upon the mountain's high peak, there are many positions and statuses, but the mason is a bystander. He is the one who crafts the stone columns that hold the earth, and he carves the images into the plaster and marble so that they may take their place in history. Creating the images is only part of his profession, as he must also represent them in a manner that is truthful and glorious, for only few men achieve both of these qualities. Mortar is the medium through which he recounts the stories he hears, and this is how the world knows of days long past. The mason mixed the plaster as he considered the power of the mortar in his hands.

He whispered under his breath, "If only all men knew their lives could be crafted in such a way."

If the mason adds too much water to his mix, a film appears on the surface and separates from the core of his plaster. It will be too weak. At the same time, if he adds too little, his mix will be difficult to turn, and too dry to add the images needed.

Upon the pillar he painted a man, who, with outstanding weight upon his back, bent down to pick up a boy. As the mix began to set, the man would be forever captured, his spirit eternally forged in cold stone, upon a cold mountain, but with fire in his soul. In his lowest moment, he chose to not yield. Instead he decided to pick up the boy who needed most to be picked up, and to not drop the weight of the world while doing so. Carved into the pillar was black armor, and in this captured moment Stelios demonstrated to the world that despite his despair and the depths through which he had to trudge, his bravery was born, grown, and cultivated inside the warrior himself. Trees withered and mountains crumbled — the world aged — but the mixture and the image stood, a pillar holding the temple of the gods. It did not fall apart, nor crack, nor bend under the immense weight. It remained. And it was not, then, the words the Myrmidon warrior spoke, but rather the actions he took in life that showed his true self, as he walked through hell and the endless darkness.

A balance of the art is what the mason searched for. A balance of the scars the Myrmidon earned on his black armor, his body, his heart, and on his soul.

Dust flew into the air and lingered as the mason clapped his hands together, and as he stepped away from the artwork, thunder erupted from the clouds and lightning tore the sky to pieces.

And, far below the pillars, a steady hand grasped the right stone.

ONLY THE DEAD HAVE SEEN THE
END OF WAR.

- PLATO

ABOUT THE AUTHOR

Liam Chambers is a Royal Canadian Air Force Officer based out of Shearwater, Nova Scotia. You can find him trail running, reading, or on the mats practicing Brazilian Jiu Jitsu. Father to an energetic two-year-old, Liam is a fitness enthusiast, completing Ironman Lake Placid, a charity event for wounded veterans where he completed 3000 pullups in 20 hours, and competing at two Military World Games in soccer. Liam recently focused some of this energy and commitment into his passion for writing.

"Scars and Black Armor" is Liam's first published novel. His favorite books include "The Virtues of War," by Steven Pressfield, and "The Alchemist" by Paulo Coelho.

www.ingramcontent.com/pod-product-compliance
Lightning Source LLC
Chambersburg PA
CBHW051509260626
47162CB00008B/2891